No More

Antoinette Foxworthy

A Russian Hill Press Book
United States • United Kingdom • Australia

Russian Hill Press

Cover Designer: John Dalessio

LCCN: 2017957267

ISBN: 978-0-9995162-0-1

To domestic violence victims—those who have the strength yet to be discovered, and those who had the strength to say no more.

"We gain strength, and courage, and confidence by each experience in which we really stop to look fear in the face ... we must do that which we think we cannot."

Eleanor Roosevelt

Hidden Fire

each morning upon waking
anguish waking with me
unshakable through the day,
sharing my bed each night,
my pillow wet with tears.

months grow into years
while paralyzed was I
by painful words, stabbing loss
absence, a gaping hole.

one day, bolstered by a stranger's words
reminded, I've a well of strength within,
power to move, move though dragging
a weight of great magnitude.

move I must.
just a first step required.
honoring the person I am
I move, trusting my inner strength,
though petrified in the process.

With slippery palms,
pounding heart, throat dry,
whole body trembles.
difficult to speak the words
that must be said out loud.

relief arrived as realization dawned.
I'm on my journey bound for the finish.
no longer helpless, but honoring,
fearlessly I make the next step
now knowing each step builds
on confidence born of the first.

as lava churns beneath volcanic craters
then explodes in fiery spectacle
within each of us,
spectacular strength awaits,
burning to be tapped.

Marilyn Dumesnil

NO MORE

ONE

HER KNEES BUCKLED AS SHE COLLAPSED IN THE chair. Her lungs seemed to be vacuumed of all air as the verdict was read. "We, the jury find the defendant, Orenthal James Simpson, not guilty in the crime of murder ..." *How could this be? This is not the right verdict. No. No.`*

Dr. Anita Stone wholeheartedly believed O.J. Simpson bludgeoned Nicole Brown Simpson and Ronald Goldman to death. She maintained her composure even though bile rumbled in her gut. She was in the breakroom at her office along with seven of her employees all transfixed to the television. There was an audible gasp as the verdict was read. Her staff, all seated in straight-back birch chairs around the rectangular lunch table, collectively stiffened and bent their heads down. Clearly, Anita wasn't the only one shocked.

She hadn't engaged in direct conversations with her employees about the trial, but she had overheard them discussing how they felt. The country was divided, along race lines, in their opinion of O.J.'s guilt or innocence. Anita had one black woman on her staff, and she suspected that staff member thought O.J. was innocent. The rest of her staff thought he was guilty. They all knew O.J. was an American hero, a football legend, and a black man, at a time when blacks were believed to be getting a raw deal by the police.

Had the prosecution done their job presenting enough evidence to convict O.J. beyond a reasonable doubt? Clearly, this jury didn't think so, but Anita was convinced that O.J. was a murderer even though the prosecution didn't prove it.

To Anita, the judicial system had failed; failed Nicole Brown Simpson, Ronald Goldman, their families, and all those suffering from domestic abuse. The light beige room became dark, the walls distorted; wavy as if they were collapsing. The air became still, stale and foul.

It felt like a vise gripped Anita's chest but she forced air into her constricted lungs once, twice. She closed her eyes, circled her head trying to relieve the tension in her neck and shoulders. Then she took another breath and slowly opened her eyes. She knew all too well how to squash her emotions, bury them deep in the earth and continue on. It was an all too common practice now. She turned toward the hallway, praying her secret was not revealed on her face or in her mannerisms. She walked out of the breakroom to see her next patient knowing that underneath her designer, long-sleeve silk blouse and white lab coat she hid bruises—bruises on her upper arms, inflicted by her husband, Daryl.

Slowing making her way down the hallway, she stopped at one of her favorite pictures. It was taken by her business partner, Dr. Thomas Kirkland, on his recent trip to Maui. Sunlit clouds mirrored on the calm surface of the Pacific Ocean. Taking in the imaginary fresh tropical air of the ocean, she pulled it down into her lungs. She relaxed her shoulders but her neck remained tight and stiff.

How had she gotten herself into this mess? How had she not seen the signs? She had never met a person so full of contradictions before like Dr. Jekyll and Mr. Hyde. She had seen the results of physical violence in her orthopedic practice and had set and pinned fractures from abusive relationships. She even studied battered wife syndrome in medical school as part of her mandatory classes but didn't fully grasp, until recently, how or why women, particularly intelligent professional women with careers, not just impoverished ones, didn't just leave their abusers. Now, she understood all too well. She was one of them.

She learned it's not about money or lack of it. It's not just about getting out of an abusive relationship. It's about getting out and not looking over your shoulder. Getting out without being too scared walking to your car after work in the dark. Getting out and not fearing for your safety or the safety of those you love. Getting out wasn't easy.

Anita had married Daryl on the rebound, months after her first marriage dissolved. He looked good on his résumé; an MBA from UC Berkeley, a member of the chamber of commerce, a successful business man who happened to be ruggedly handsome too. His thick mane of wavy caramel-colored hair was just long and unruly enough to look sexy. It projected both a naughty guy and an I-clean-up-well one. He stood six feet two inches tall and proud. His mustache was neatly trimmed, his jaw chiseled and strong, a Tom Selleck twin. He wooed her off her feet promising unconditional love.

On this day, October 3, 1995, after her last patient, Anita hurried to her car careful not to seem rushed. She pulled out of the parking lot and drove around the corner and opened her door. Thinking what the O.J. Simpson verdict of not guilty meant to battered women everywhere, she vomited the contents of her stomach and bile into the street. When she was certain the heaving had stopped, she shut the door, sipped stale water from the water bottle in her car, wiped her mouth with a tissue, sat up straight, and headed home.

Her stomach felt as if a roller derby was happening inside her, complete with the elbows in the ribs and the racing to catch up to your opponent only to keep going around and around in circles.

Her saving grace tonight was that Daryl was out of town on business and she did not have to face him. She didn't have to face anyone except the mirror.

She slipped into her pajamas at 7:30 p.m., made a cup of herbal tea, and sat in front of the television mesmerized by the coverage of the O.J. Simpson trial. With bleary eyes, she watched over and over his reaction to the not-guilty verdict. There was a smirk on his face. She saw it. *How dare he?*

She was feeling trapped and embarrassed and, after today's verdict, very, very alone and afraid. She couldn't believe she had gotten into this mess. She wanted to get out; get off this roller coaster of ups and downs. But how? The plan she made with the counselor didn't seem right. Instead, she wanted to discuss their situation again with Daryl, hoping he would understand. She didn't just want to leave one day. She felt like a complete loser. How could she get out with her dignity intact? Who could help her? She told everyone how perfect Daryl was for her. She'd lied for so long to everyone including herself.

Anita was startled from her thoughts when the phone rang. She let it go to the answering machine and heard Daryl's angry voice. "Anita, it's your husband. I would have expected you to be home by now. Call me back." Click.

She took a deep breath. She didn't want to talk to him but knew he would call back shortly. She sighed, went over the kitchen sink and got a glass of water.

As she was walking back to the counter to pick up the phone it rang again. She answered it.

"Hello."

"I just called you and you didn't answer."

She shook her head. "Daryl, I was just picking up the phone to call you back."

"I see. Why didn't you answer the first time?"

"This is ridiculous. I've had a long day. Can't I even go to the bathroom in peace?" Anita forgave herself for the little lie.

"Okay. I'm sorry. How was your day?"

Anita took a sip of water, rubbed the back of her neck, and responded. "Honestly, I've had a trying day. One patient in the hospital isn't responding to the antibiotics, but I don't really want to talk about that. I was just microwaving my dinner. *Another lie but anything to keep from irritating him.* 'Did you have a good day?"

"Yes, it was wonderful. I miss you."

"Honestly, can we talk tomorrow night? I had a miserable day."

"Don't you miss me?"

"Yes, of course. It's just that I'm very hungry and I need to get to bed. I have early rounds."

"Okay, then. Good night." Daryl hung up the phone.

Anita knew from the abrupt ending of the call that Daryl was irritated. She didn't care. She placed the phone back in its cradle. He didn't even mention the O.J. verdict. Of course he didn't. *I just need to get something in my stomach and go to bed, forget.*

That night Anita tossed and turned. During the wee hours of the morning, she finally fell asleep only to be awakened by nightmares. She bolted upright in bed; her throat desert dry and constricted. It felt like a dead lizard was stuck in her throat.

"This sucks," she said quietly. "I have to come up with a different plan to get out. I'm a medical doctor for Christ's sakes. I've defied the odds many times in my life, but I don't know how to do this. It's not like I can go to the local shelter which the counselor suggested and ask for help. In this small town I'd be recognized. I'd be humiliated. What would patients say if they heard their doctor was being abused by her husband? What would my medical partner Thomas think? I'd be known as the doctor who was being abused. I'd lose business for sure."

Anita scanned the tidy dark room. Tears trickled down her cheeks and into the corners of her lips. "Come on, Anita, you can do this. There is a way out and you'll find it. There are people who can help you." She laid her wet cheek on the pillow, closed her eyes and thought of her mother, her dear mother.

Anita was startled when the alarm clock blared at 6:00 a.m. *What was I dreaming?* She couldn't remember but her throat was no longer tight. She was composed. *I think I was talking to Mom in the dream. We were on a beach. Something she said to me gave me a new resolve. What is it, Mom?* She put her head back on the pillow wishing for another moment of clarity in the dream. She couldn't remember the details, but, she had a different outlook than yesterday. She didn't have a plan, but she knew she had to get out and get out quickly.

Daryl returned home from his business trip that day. She tiptoed around him for the next three days, careful not to upset him. She was worried that the verdict would give Daryl license to hit her knowing O.J. could get away with murder. Secretly she was churning over plans to leave. She spent long hours at the office and Daryl was growing impatient. Anita agreed to be home early for dinner the next night. When she arrived Daryl, a scotch in one hand, handed her a chilled glass of Rombauer Chardonnay.

He had planned a casual, romantic evening and had made one of her favorite meals—leek infused poached salmon with saffron rice and honey glazed baby carrots. The table was set with Wedgewood china and crystal wine glasses with a bouquet of long stemmed, pale pink roses in the center. The soft flicker from six tall white candles beneath the dimmed Bellini chandelier created a dreamy setting. Soft jazz played in the background. She thought, this guy is really romantic tonight. *I bet O.J. was too. Remember, Anita, what life is like with Daryl. You've got to get out.*

Daryl finished off his scotch while plating the dinner and poured himself another one before they sat down. The dinner was delicious; quiet and peaceful. They chatted about his recent big sales deal in Oregon. He seemed very pleased with himself. Daryl switched from scotch to wine midway through dinner.

When they finished with their meal he got up from his chair and sauntered over to Anita. He stood behind her, placed his hands on her shoulders and gently rubbed them. She tried to relax. Then, he kissed her on the neck and suggested they leave the dirty dishes on the table and head upstairs. Anita gingerly pulled away. "I need to take a bath," she said aloud but thought, maybe he'll be passed out when I'm out of the tub.

That's all it took for Daryl to switch to Mr. Hyde. He exploded and lit into her, pushing and shoving her, hitting her arms and chest. She ran upstairs begging him to stop. He followed two stairs at a time and slammed their bedroom door after them. It rattled in the hinges. He hit her repeatedly in the face. As best she could, she dodged his punches. She pleaded with him, all to no avail.

At last, it was time for Anita to make her move. She tightly balled up her fist, drew it back and with all the power of her rage threw a punch. She missed Daryl and hit the bedroom door, smashing a hole through the hollow door, breaking her hand and Daryl's concentration. He stopped, stunned. The victim had become the aggressor. Fear now in his eyes. She shoved him aside with strength from the racing adrenaline, pulled opened the bedroom door with her good hand, and ran downstairs.

As Anita dashed out of the house she had the foresight to grab her purse from the entryway table. Out of instinct she grabbed for it with her right hand only to be reminded of the searing pain radiating up that arm from the punch. She snatched her purse with her good left hand before she was out the door into the dark night.

TWO

SHE DIDN'T SHUT THE DOOR. SHE DIDN'T LOOK back. She just ran. Anita raced down her tree-lined street in flight mode, pumped with adrenaline-fueled rage, her long wavy chestnut hair floating wildly behind her. Her heart thumped violently in her chest. The night seemed eerily quiet. All she heard was her strained breathing and the clop, clop of her stiff low heeled shoes on the sidewalk. She slowed down slightly for a second and nervously peered over her shoulder. She could not see him coming after her, at least, not on foot. Her fear was that he'd try to catch her in his car, but there were no cars coming either. She continued on. She rounded the corner of her street and had a decision to make—go west toward the only outlet to and from her neighborhood or turn east back toward the development where she presumed Daryl would not go if he were looking for her.

East. *He won't be looking for me there. But, what will I do?*

She fled around the corner. When she was fairly certain he was not following her, she ducked behind a large rosemary bush to catch her breath and think.

For months she had been thinking of ways to get out of her marriage peacefully. However since the O.J. verdict, she was more determined than ever. It became clear to her that men can get away with abusing their wives, even killing them. This was her breaking point. She had followed the case closely knowing that Nicole had left O.J. and that their relationship had been volatile. She wanted to get out of her marriage as peacefully and as soon as possible, but she knew Daryl would not agree to any of the conditions or scenarios she had come up with. This was one scenario she hadn't thought through; escaping on foot, at night, with a broken hand, a punched-up face and only her purse and the clothes on her back.

Now what? Then, in a moment of relief, a respite from what had just happened, she smiled. *I'm glad I've been working out, and I wore my practical low-heeled shoes and loose pants to work today.*

The escalating pain throbbing in her hand brought her back to reality. She was frightened. She was alone. She cried silently. Her sobs were interrupted by the ringing of her cell phone in her purse—probably Daryl calling her. *I'm not going to answer and listen to his faked apologies. Not this time.* When the noise stopped, she carefully reached into her purse with her left hand, and dialed Dr. Thomas Kirkland, the one person she knew in town who would protect her, repair her broken hand, and offer her the guidance she needed to get back on track.

ANITA HAD MET THOMAS WHEN SHE APPLIED FOR the position as a second orthopedic surgeon in his office. He contacted her and asked her to come to Nesport, a quaint town in Northern California, population 10,000, to interview as another orthopedist. As she walked into his waiting room she thought, what am I getting into? *This office is ancient. I'm just beginning my practice. I'm young and I want a modern new look with the most up-to-date equipment.* But, when Dr. Thomas Kirkland came out into the waiting room, he methodically extended his burly hand and greeted her. His chocolate voice comforted her as though he was a long lost grandfather.

"Anita?" he asked. Here was the man behind the voice that had persuaded her to come to this interview. He had an uncanny resemblance to her grandfather with a square face, distinguished jawline, sparkling blue eyes, and graying thin hair. He was slightly taller than she and stood with an unassuming yet purposeful stance. My sweet, dear grandfather reincarnate, she thought.

"Yes." Anita extended her hand.

Thomas clasped her hand with both of his. "Welcome. I'm Dr. Kirkland—Thomas. It is my pleasure to finally meet you in person after all our phone conversations. Please come in." Dr. Kirkland gestured with his arm in a big circle. "This is my humble, yet, I fear, outdated waiting room. I've been meaning to remodel and my wife has been on my case to get the reception area into the current century, but I'm afraid I've put esthetics on the back burner in my growing practice. This is my receptionist, Jillian."

Anita extended her hand. "Hello."

"May I offer you a cup of tea?" Jillian asked as she stood and shook Anita's hand.

"I'll make it, Jillian. Thanks for offering," Thomas said.

"Tea?"

"Yes, that would be nice."

Thomas and Anita walked together down the stark beige hallway. It smelled of band aids, sticky tape and disinfectant. When they arrived at Thomas' office he said, "Please sit down. I'll be right back."

She sat on one of the comfy, jade green chairs noticing the rich maroon wallpaper covering the wall behind his enormous desk. His office didn't resemble the bleakness of the waiting room at all. On the wall hung a magnificent painting of a dazzling sun peeking through oversized palm trees, the same lush color as the chairs, with a cobalt blue ocean in the background. The sun, still low on the horizon, illuminated the trees waking them up to the possibilities of the day. However, Dr. Kirkland's huge desk seemed so out dated in these surroundings. The size of the Cherrywood was so out of proportion to the room, taking up more than half the space. It was nicked and somewhat dull; four huge legs supported what looked like webbed duck feet—an albatross in the room. It was neatly piled with patient charts and a picture of him and, presumably, his wife also surrounded by palm trees. His diploma was professionally framed and proudly displayed on the side wall next to the neatly arranged medical books and journals in the bookcases. Dr. Thomas R. Kirkland had graduated from Stanford Medical School before Anita was born.

"Here is our tea," Thomas announced as he returned holding two steaming green ceramic mugs. Anita turned toward him and accepted her tea.

His demeanor and relaxed voice made her feel comfortable and welcome. He reminded her so much of her beloved grandfather, Harry. He, like Thomas rarely got rattled or upset no matter what the circumstances. Working with Thomas had proven to be a perfect decision for her. Anita grew exponentially as a doctor under Thomas's tutelage. The first year they formed a strong bond between teacher and student; mentor and sponge. Anita became more patient, calmer and more relaxed after working alongside Thomas. He was very precise and method- ical in surgery no matter how complicated or difficult the procedure. When he had to give upsetting news, his words instilled confidence that he was doing everything he could to help his patients.

By the second year, as her confidence, skills and practical knowledge grew, Anita could see Thomas backing away from his role as adviser and letting her work more on her own. He respected the doctor she had become. She even convinced him to expand and redecorate the waiting room, but he would not let go of his obsolete desk. "It keeps me grounded," he explained. "It was my father's desk. I feel his presence near me, especially when I'm working late or struggling with a complicated case. He used this desk in his office for forty-two years. He was a calm man—methodically calm and wise. He was a general practitioner here in town. I miss him."

As the night swarmed down on her and the agonizing pain both in her hand and in her soul erupted, she had dialed the most trusted friend she had in this town.

After three rings she heard that familiar, gentleman-like, smooth chocolate voice, "Hello … Hello?"

THREE

ANITA INHALED DEEPLY, THEN EXHALED ALL THE air from her lungs, a technique she had learned as an intern while facing urgent situations which required her to be the calm in the eye of the storm. After she released her clenched jaw and allowed her constricted, scratchy throat to swallow, she said, "Thomas. It's Anita. I need your help."

"Anita, what's going on?"

"I need you to come pick me up, now." Her eyes darted back and forth, scanning for signs of Daryl.

"Of course. Are you all right? Has there been an accident? Where are you? Let me get a piece of paper and write down the address."

"I don't have the exact address." Then, she took another deep, cleansing breath. "You know how to get to my house?"

"Yes."

"Instead of driving west on Adams Circle, drive east when you get into my tract. Then, make the first left turn onto Jefferson. I'm at the second house on the left."

Sounding confused, Thomas said, "Sure, I'll be there in ten minutes. But Anita, what has happened? Why are you at a neighbor's house?"

"Just come. Thomas, one other thing ..." She gulped air through her mouth like she had just popped up from being submerged under water for a long time. "If you see Daryl or his red Porsche, please don't stop. Just come get me."

"This doesn't sound good, Anita. Did you have a fight? Are you all right?"

"No, it isn't good and I'm not alright. I need your help." She scrunched deeper behind the rosemary bush.

"Okay. Yes, I'll be there within ten minutes. I'm on my way."

BARBARA KIRKLAND, A RETIRED HIGH SCHOOL principal, knew fear when she saw it on her husband's face. Thomas frowned and paced the room, scanning for his keys and wallet and headed for the door. This was not a medical call. This was a different type of emergency.

Barbara followed him around. "I'll get your coat. What's happened? Where are you going?"

He snatched the coat from her hands on his way

out the door and turned to her. "It's the call, Barbara. The call we both knew would eventually come from Anita. Daryl's done something to her. I just know it. I just don't know what yet."

"Is Anita all right? Should I come with you? Where is she?" She buzzed around the kitchen like a fly would in the window trying to escape.

"I'm going to go get her. I need you to stay here. I don't know where Daryl is and I don't want you in any danger. I'll call you as soon as I can."

Rapid-fire questions escaped from Barbara's mouth. "What about the police? Shouldn't we be calling the police? Where are you going? Where is Anita?"

"Barbara, stay calm." He gave her a quick hug. "I've got to go. I'll call you. I love you." He hurried into the garage and opened his car door and turned to face her. She was massaging her hands together; shifting her weight from side to side. "She's in her neighborhood. I'll be home as soon as I can."

SHIVERING AND HUNKERED DOWN LIKE A SCARED baby rabbit, thoughts swirled in Anita's head. *Oh my god, what have I done? What should I do now? Think logically, Dr. Stone. What has to happen next? What's your most critical need?* Her medical training kicked in. *I need to be safe. It's the most critical and only thing I need at this moment. What do I need to do to ensure my safety?* She crouched lower behind the bush and assessed her injuries. *Nothing life threatening.*

She wondered if Daryl was still at home or if he was trying to find her. She realized how much her face hurt. Her left eye was sore and throbbing. Daryl's punches had landed on her face and left shoulder. She had dodged most of his blows but winced as she remembered the stinging pain when his fist landed on her face. Gingerly, she reached up and touched her eye. She felt the swelling in the soft tissue of her eyelid. *Please, not another black eye and no permanent eye damage.*

Thoughts echoed in her skull, none were clear. All were jumbled. *I wonder if I intentionally hit the door earlier when I balled up my fist or if, in my fury, I just missed. Did the Hippocratic Oath phrase, "do no harm" will my fist to miss Daryl's chin? The oath surely was not referring to protecting yourself. He is not my patient. I was defending myself from a crazed, insensible man.*

How long has it been since I called Thomas? Eight, ten minutes. I can't see my watch in the dark and I don't dare turn on the light on my phone.

Silence. No cars passed by. No one on foot. She was relieved that Daryl wasn't coming but also concerned that Thomas was taking so long. *Wait. I hear a motor.* Headlights were coming. *What if it's Daryl? How will I tell if it's Thomas's car?* She listened for the shifting sound of Daryl's Porsche coming down the street. This was not it. Relief again.

"Too long. This is taking too long," she murmured to herself. *Patience, Dr. Stone.* The car passed. It wasn't Thomas's Mercedes. The headlights were too close together.

Finally, after what seemed like an hour of quiet and darkness, she heard an engine and saw headlights as a car rounded the corner. As it slowed and grew nearer, Anita recognized Thomas's car and bolted out of the shrubbery just as he pulled up to the curb. He leaned over to the passenger's door and opened it.

She scurried, almost flying into the seat along with the cool night air. She flung herself into the seat. Instinctively she reached to close the car door with her right hand only to have the searing pain startle her. She reached over and pulled it shut with her left hand.

"What's happened?" Thomas's brow was furled tightly, his jaw clenched.

"Let's get out of here, first."

"We should call the police. Your eye is practically swollen shut. Anita, we need to call 911."

"Thomas, don't. "No … no. That will only inflame him." Her body shook.

"Daryl did this to you, didn't he?"

She slumped in the seat. Tears poured down her face.

"Anita, I'm so sorry. I'll get you out of here. Are you injured anywhere else?"

"Yes, I'm pretty sure I have a boxer's fracture on my right hand. I heard it crack when I hit the door. And, I don't know the extent of the damage to my eye. I need X-rays to see how severely I'm injured. I thought about going to the office but then the lights would be on and Daryl would know I was there. I think we should just go to the ER but I don't want anyone to know about this."

"Let's get to a safe place and we'll figure out the rest." He put the car in gear and headed down the street.

"Please hurry. Daryl's in a blind rage. He's dangerous, Thomas, and he'll be looking for me. He might even have his gun. He's crazy."

"A gun? Oh my god. This is nothing to mess around with."

Anita was shaking uncontrollably.

Thomas made a U-turn in the next driveway, and raced along Adams Circle toward Washington Street just as a red Porsche flew by in the opposite direction.

FOUR

ANITA GLIMPSED DARYL'S PORSCHE AND SLOUCHED deeper in the seat, her shaking more violent, earthquake-like, and panicked that Daryl might have seen her. Thomas gripped the steering wheel, veins in his neck bulged, eyes laser-focused on the road, sped toward the Emergency Room.

"Did he see me?"

"No, Anita," Thomas reassured her. "He doesn't know my car. You're okay now. Please stay calm. Take some deep breaths. I'll get you to safety. I promise."

Anita's body slid further toward the floor but was constricted by the seatbelt. Her eyes twitched, her legs numb, she gulped for air. Her stomach, gripped in a vise, kept her vomit down.

"You know Barbara and I think of you as the

daughter we never had. I'm here for you."

She peered up as Thomas tensed over the steering wheel; his eyes moist under his glasses. Warmth flushed in her veins. *Daughter? Like a daughter to me? That's what he said.* She hadn't heard those words in so long.

She closed her eyes, heart thumping in her chest and thought back to her childhood.

I CAN'T REMEMBER MY BIOLOGICAL FATHER EVER calling me daughter. He left when I was only eight years old. He left us like discarded worn shoes buried deep in a closet. He left us and started a whole new family while he was still married to Mom. We were both devastated when we found out, betrayed. At first I thought it was my fault but after months of therapy, which Mom insisted we both attend, I realized that my father's leaving was not focused on me. My feelings were jumbled, like random pick-up sticks. I never knew which one I would pick up at any given time. I hated my dad for leaving but I still wanted him to be my dad. I still wanted to be his daughter; to be loved and twirled in the air and be read bedtime stories, but I was angry, lonely and frustrated. *What went wrong?* I didn't know. I was very mixed-up. Mom was too.

My father's new family included my half-sister, Monica. After she was born Pete—how I refer to my father now—barely acknowledged my existence. He and his other family moved to Nevada when Monica was one year old. It was then that my mom changed our surnames from Hancock, which was Pete's surname and her married name, back to her maiden name, Stone. Pete made no objections.

It was my mother, Louise, who became my rock after Pete left. I was her only child and I worshipped my mom, clung to her tightly. She was always there; helping with science projects, cheering from the bleachers at all my soccer games, wiping tears from my cheeks after my prom date cancelled. My mother was my best ally and best friend.

After Pete's abrupt departure, I hid in books making them my new reality. It was my escape, my retreat. I rarely brought friends over, embarrassed by our sparse surroundings in our little apartment. Eventually, all my reading and studying paid off and, in high school I was offered a scholarship to San Jose State. From there I went to Stanford Medical School.

Throughout college I lived at home and remained more focused on my studies, shunning the usual college social activities and parties. I used to think, "Who lives at home with their mother throughout college?" But Mom needed me and I needed Mom.

Letting go and moving out when I went to medical school was difficult. Not a week went by that I didn't talk to Mom. I shared everything with her, from my insecurities to my accomplishments. I finally blossomed at Stanford Medical School. I was interested in boys and they in me, but they weren't my priority until I met Jack Bowman, a fellow medical student who uplifted my spirits.

Jack came from a normal family with a Mom and Dad and Sunday dinners. His family lived in San Mateo and we visited often. I felt like I finally had a family. They included my mother in their dinners. Mom loved Jack too. She credited him with pulling me out of my shell and into the outside world. Jack became my husband when we both finished our internships at UCSF. Mom was proud of me and so happy for our marriage. Jack wanted me to take his surname, Bowman, but after long discussions I decided not to. I thought it might be too complicated having two doctor Bowmans in the same household.

Jack and I both returned to Stanford for our residencies. Our bedroom was our life. We were either making love, eating or studying, all in a tiny bedroom with its king sized bed. The bed took up most of the room. Jack often joked that, if I was sleeping, he had to leap over me from just inside the bedroom door in order to get into bed. Usually, when he hoped over me he woke me up.

Things were humming along for Jack and me. We discussed having children. We had been married three years and built up our medical practices.

Then, I got the call from a somber, unknown female voice.

"Dr. Anita Stone?"

"Yes."

"I'm Nurse Barnwell, an ER nurse at Washington Hospital in Fremont. Your mother is Louise Stone?"

"Yes." I closed my eyes. Something was wrong, very wrong. I could tell by the tone of the nurse's voice. Goosebumps prickled my arms. My throat instantly went desert dry.

"Louise Stone has been in a car accident."

My thoughts garbled in my mushy brain. "Is she all right?" My tongue felt like sandpaper scraping against a dry sidewalk. My heart pounded so hard in my chest wall I thought it might break my rib cage. *Calm down and breathe.* "Listen," I prompted myself and rocked side to side on my feet.

Calmly, the nurse continued. "She's been injured. We have her heavily sedated but she told us your phone number and name before we gave her pain meds. She's getting X-rays now. I would suggest you come to the hospital as soon as possible."

It was so hard to hear with my heart hammering so loudly in my chest. My heart leapt into my throat, heavy and constricting. "What are her injuries?"

"Dr. Stone, we're still assessing her at this time, but we'd like you to come to the emergency room."

Heat radiated up my torso. My shoulders stiffened. "I'll be there as soon as I can. I'm leaving now. It will take me about thirty minutes."

Thirty minutes was too long. I never got to say goodbye to my mother. A damn drunk driver robbed her of her golden years and left a gaping, jagged hole in my chest. The drunk disintegrated my security blanket and a persistent gray cloud descended around me.

FIVE

ANITA'S LIFE BECAME A BLUR AFTER HER MOM'S death. For months Anita had nightmares that she was in a row boat in a hurricane being tossed into jagged rocks. She couldn't get the oars in the water. She had no rudder.

She went to therapy alone. She and Jack went to therapy, but Anita just kept pushing Jack further away. In nine months, her marriage to Jack dissolved. She didn't want to love him anymore. She was convinced that when she loves someone they leave or abandon her anyway, just like her father and her mother. She didn't feel worthy. Instead of working through her grief with her husband she worked non-stop, devoting all her time to her orthopedic practice. She gave all she had to strangers who counted on her to fix them, to heal them, to make them better instead of healing herself or her marriage.

A year after the divorce, she met Daryl Davidson at a charity event, a bad boy who flirted and drank too much but piled on the attention. He was naughty and reckless, the center of attention. Anita thought he was just aloof enough for her not to get in too deep. She could have thrilling sex, which she was craving again, but leave in the morning, not get attached. After three dates she knew she was wrong. She started falling for Daryl.

ANITA SILENTLY PRAYED. *NO MORE HURT, PLEASE God. No more hurt. Wake me from this terrible dream.*

Thomas parked in a space reserved for doctors near the Emergency Room entrance. He gently tapped Anita on her shoulder, bringing her back to reality.

"Anita, it's okay now. We're here at the ER. Let's get you in and have a good look at you. You're safe now, sweetie. Come with me." Anita looked up at Thomas with his easy demeanor like soft boiled eggs and his calming velvet voice.

She slowly nodded and sighed. Gradually she sat up, still guarded and fretful; anxious to get into the hospital but afraid of all that had happened, begging for an end to this nightmare.

Thomas scurried around to the passenger's door and opened it. He helped Anita out of the car, shut the door, and the two of them entered the ER together.

SIX

DRESSED IN A HOSPITAL GOWN AND NESTLED IN familiar surroundings, Anita's tense shoulders relaxed. Thomas stood next to her as the ER doctor examined her. Her eye was swollen shut, the delicate skin inflamed with fluid. The pain in her eye had increased but the dull ache about her chin and shoulder was something she had, unfortunately, become accustomed to. Her right hand throbbed and hurt a great deal. It was broken. She had heard it crack when she hit it on the door.

The metal rings of the curtains surrounding her makeshift room clinked together each time the nurse or doctor entered. Anita had never noticed the sound of the rings on the makeshift room when she was attending to patients in the ER but now the sound was grating, irritating like cats fighting in the middle of the night. The muscles in her jaw tightened; her guard back on alert, voices bombarded her with questions she didn't want to answer. Finally, everyone was outside her room. She guessed that they were checking X-rays and consulting with an ophthalmologist.

The annoying clink of the rings signaled another visitor. A police officer appeared standing proud in his uniform and asked if she could answer a few questions about the evening.

Her mind swirled with anxieties like a burst of wind scattering dry dead leaves that could not land. Her stomach felt like he had punched it. Her brain was bombarded with lights like a psychedelic Aurora Borealis.

I didn't call the police. Did the ER doctor? Did Thomas? What if I tell him Daryl did this to me, will he go to jail? What will he do to me then when he gets out? What am I going to tell him? I can handle this on my own. I don't want to talk to this macho guy standing in front of me with his gun holstered to his belt.

She felt a rustle of breath squeeze through her constricted lungs. The pit of her stomach felt like the tip of a rod after you've pulled off the roasted marshmallow from the camp fire.

Thomas appeared from behind the officer. He came toward her and gently wrapped his arm around her shoulder. He said, "Anita, this is bigger than you can handle."

"But, Thomas," she protested. "You don't understand." Her back became stiff, board-like.

Turning to the policeman, Thomas said. "Please give us a few minutes."

The police officer left the examination room.

Thomas gently sat next to her on the hospital bed. He wrapped his arm tighter around her shoulders. "Anita, please, I would like to tell you something."

"Thomas, I can't tell the police. You don't understand." She was vehement, angry. Her heart was thumping in her chest. Her lungs filled with cement not allowing air to penetrate. She turned her head away from him and stared at the blood pressure machine. She heard the incessant beeping from another room.

"Anita, please," Thomas's voice came out as soft as a baby blanket. "I may not understand Daryl. I may not understand exactly what you are going through, but I'd like to tell you what I do know. Look at me Anita. Please, look at me." Slowly, she turned, inched her chin upward, and looked into his calm eyes.

His voice came out in the sing-song rhythm of a lullaby. "You don't have to hide anymore. The facade has crumbled. You don't deserve what is happening to you."

"But, I've finally decided to leave him, to divorce him. There's no need to get the police involved." Her words came out harsh and raspy. Her eyes were steely, hard as marbles.

"Anita, just because you want a divorce doesn't mean Daryl will walk away. Please listen to me. I do not know everything, but here's what I do know for sure." He paused, letting Anita calm down and focus on his words. "Situations like this are not easy. I've seen patients come back year after year with similar injuries. It's time to stop this roller coaster and get to some quiet, stable ground. You are devoted to healing and caring for your patients. You are now my patient and I'm going to help you. Trust me. It's time to heal. However, this is a dangerous situation, one we cannot handle on our own. The police are here to help and protect you too."

Anita finally felt the cement melt from her lungs and took a deep breath.

He paused and looked into her eyes; calm eyes, sleeping baby calm. His voice was creamy smooth.

"There is something uniquely special about you, Anita."

Anita eyes welled up. The hummingbird-paced fluttering in her chest eased.

Thomas continued, "I knew it when I first interviewed you. I believed in you then and nothing has challenged that belief. We are both here for a reason. Nothing is a coincidence. We're part of a bigger plan. We don't have to understand everything. We are doctors, practicing orthopedics together for a reason. Hell, you're even in the ER right now for a reason. Some of life's lessons are difficult." Anita lowered her chin to her chest. "Anita, you trust me don't you?"

"Of course."

"Then let me, let Barbara and I, help you through this. Sometimes we don't know why or how we are in a situation, but I have learned that there are no mistakes, only opportunities to grow and learn and understand.

"Life is difficult particularly when you are walking through quicksand instead of beside it. But, I am here with you. Take my hand." He extended his hand toward her.

He halted and let her take in what he was saying. Slowly she reached toward his big burly hand. Tenderly he closed his fingers around hers clasping them firmly. Her entire body softened as she relaxed in the comfort of his words. His warmth radiated up her arm. Tears welled in the corners of her eyes.

Thomas continued, a soft smile on his lips. "The universe is telling us that it's time. It's time you began believing in yourself as much as I believe in you. You can do this. Barbara and I will be with you every step of the way."

He wrapped his arms around her. She quietly cried, wetting his neatly pressed white shirt. Tears for her mother, whom she desperately missed; tears for the little girl whose father had abandoned her at eight; tears for her failed marriage to Jack, the loving husband she pushed away; tears of pain deep in her soul. Jumbo tears locked up for a very long time.

Dr. Thomas Kirkland, with his superman-like vision, had seen through her steel wall and finally broke it down.

The one living person I admire the most, still believes in me.

Anita sat upright. Her caved spine straightened as she looked into Thomas's caring eyes. "Thank you, Thomas. Thank you. I'll talk to the police now."

SEVEN

OFFICER MORRISON, WITH HIS GRAYING TEMPLES and cocoa-brown eyes, returned. Awkwardly he sat in the hard blue vinyl chair next to Anita's hospital bed. He quietly asked her questions about the incident, carefully writing in his notebook. He knew he walked a fine line trying to get as much information as possible from her yet careful not to upset her to the point that she was too scared to reveal, even to him, what had happened.

He had seen way too many of these cases in the emergency room over the years. He also know that the police could only do so much to help these victims who were often too afraid to press charges or even speak to them for fear of retaliation from their abuser.

ANITA, TAPPING HER KNEES GENTLY TOGETHER,

her head tipped down, haltingly explained that she and her husband had gotten into a fight. He had repeatedly punched her. She didn't reveal much more than that. She didn't tell him about hitting the door or that the violence had been going on for months.

After telling the officer what happened in the house that night Anita didn't want to talk anymore. A steel-gray fog enveloped her brain. It prevented her from concentrating. *Was it the pain medication finally setting in?* She barely listened as Morrison explained that there were places she could go to get help and things she could do to get away. It was all white noise. Her head throbbed, her eye oozed, and the pain in her hand escalated with even the slightest movement.

"Dr. Stone? Dr. Stone?" Her eyes were glassy. "You can file charges against your husband. I would encourage you to do so. You don't want him to do this to you again. It could even get worse than this. Let us help you. You don't deserve this."

"But, will it mean that I have to testify?"

"Most likely, at some point, but that's down the road."

"No, you don't understand. I can't do that. Don't you see? Look at what just happened with Nicole Brown Simpson. She's dead and she certainly didn't deserve what she got either. I don't want to make Daryl mad." Her words came out like darts toward Officer Morrison. "I've seen him full of rage and I don't want to ... to see him like that again. Let me sleep on this." She shook her head. Slowly she reclined on the bed and closed her eyes. Her next words came out in whispers. "I'm in so much pain right now. I don't know what's going on with my hand or my eye. Let me talk to you tomorrow. I'm tired."

Officer Morrison sighed. Anita waved her hand toward him signaling she was done with their conversation but he continued probing gently.

"What about an emergency restraining order?"

"Right now I just want to find out the extent of my injuries. I'm not ready for any restraining order." She closed her eyes. *What if Daryl finds out I told the police? What will he do?*

"Do you have a safe place to go tonight?"

Anita responded with her eyes closed and her head resting on the pillow. "Yes ... yes, I do." She nodded, although she didn't know where she was going. "Thank you. I'm going to rest now."

Officer Morrison placed his card with a case number on it onto the aluminum tray near her bed and told her to call him if she needed anything further. He assured her that he would help walk her through the process.

Anita had questions for the officer but she didn't want to ask. *What was going to happen to Daryl now? Would they arrest him even if I don't file charges? God, now what?* She really didn't want to know. She just wanted to go, disappear and pretend none of this had ever happened. She was so embarrassed, a medical doctor, the victim of domestic abuse. She wondered how she had let this happen to her.

The curtain rattled leaving Anita alone with her thoughts, her shame and her pain, but there was also a sense of relief. The cat was out of the bag, her secret uncovered. *No more hiding behind long sleeve blouses. No more excuses.*

Then, another jangle of the curtain rings as the consulting ophthalmologist, Dr. Andy Chen, entered the room. Anita peered up at her colleague. "I guess you never thought you'd see me here?"

"No, Anita, I didn't, but I need to look at your eye." Gingerly she sat up.

"No need to sit up. I can examine you lying down." Dr. Chen walked near the bed and extended his hand. Anita shook it. Her palm was clammy.

"What exactly happened, Anita?"

"Well," she took a huge sigh. "I got hit in the face with a flying fist."

"I'm so sorry. Who would want to punch you?"

"Um … my husband."

"Oh, Anita." His voice trailed off. His mannerisms back in doctor mode. "Let me examine your eye."

I don't want to answer any more questions, she thought, but I know I should. Still wrapped in the shroud of embarrassment, she wrenchingly told him about all the punches from her husband. Tears formed in the corner of her good eye. Dr. Chen gingerly examined her left one and ordered a CT scan to determine the extent of her injury.

Waiting. There's so much waiting in the ER. Anita felt sympathetic to her patients now. It's a long wait when you're hurt and anxiously waiting for a diagnosis. It's even longer when you're afraid.

The annoying clanking and then the curtains opened yet again. Barbara, with her thick, short snow-white hair, which always looked like she had just stepped out of the hair salon, was dressed in pale blue designer sweats. She ambled to Anita's bed, bent down and gingerly wrapped her warm arms around her.

Anita smiled at her kind, familiar face.

"Anita, I'm so sorry. Thomas called me. We're here for you, honey. How are you doing?"

"Not well, as you can see." Salty tears formed in the corners of Anita's eyes.

Barbara hugged her. "What a mess, Barbara. I'm pretty worried about my eye but Andy is taking care of me. He'll fix me up. My hand hurts like hell. I think it's a boxer's fracture."

"I'm so thankful that you finally are getting away from Daryl. Thomas and I knew something wasn't right but ..." Barbara paused allowing time for her words to sink deeper. "Did you finally hit Daryl back? I hope so and I hope you walloped him."

"No, I tried but I missed. I hit the door and punched a hole through it. I'm pretty strong, you know."

"Yes. Yes, you're very strong, stronger than you think."

Now, wrapped comfortably in Barbara's motherly arms, Anita fell silent with the events of the evening replaying in her mind. She didn't want to talk about it anymore. She didn't want to answer any more questions. She just wanted all the pain; all the hurt, both emotionally and physically to go away. She wanted to sleep. Her mind was puzzled and groggy.

DR. CHEN FINALLY CAME BACK GREETING BOTH Anita and Barbara. He had met Barbara Kirkland on several occasions when the doctors and their wives got together. He told Anita the CT scan revealed small, minimally displaced fractures to her left orbit but no apparent eye damage that would require surgery.

"I want to see you in my office for a follow-up appointment. You are going to look a lot worse with a whopping black eye before you look better." He continued, directing his comments toward Barbara. "Are you going to be with her?"

"Yes." Barbara nodded.

"Apply cold packs on her eye twenty minutes on and twenty minutes off for the next few days, when she's awake of course. I suggest she rest and take it easy."

He turned back toward Anita, "Do us all a favor and stay away from fast flying fists. Stay far away, Anita," he reiterated while gently taking her hand into his.

"I will, Andy. Thanks for taking a look at my eye."

"You're welcome. I'll see you in the office in a couple days. If you start having double vision or any problems, come in earlier. Do you need a prescription for Percocet or will Thomas give you one?"

"I'm good. Thomas has already taken care of that."

"Take care of yourself. If you have any questions, any at all, don't hesitate to call."

Anita nodded and smiled. "Thank you Andy."

Dr. Chen pushed the curtain aside and departed.

Thomas returned with Anita's hand X-Rays and held them up in the light for her to see. Indeed, Anita was right about the boxer's fracture. Her fifth metacarpal bone had moved out of normal alignment. They both agreed that no surgery was needed, but she would have to be in a cast for about six weeks to allow the bones to properly heal.

"Anita, I will pick up your patient load while you're recovering. Don't worry about that now."

Barbara, who was still in the room, teasingly added, "He's been pacing around the house on Mondays and Fridays following me around since he semi-retired. There's only so much golf he can play, plus the weather is getting much cooler and he's really only a fair-weather golfer. This will give him something to do, and I'll have time to brush up on my golf game while he isn't around."

Thomas said, "Let's get you in your cast, Doctor,

and get you going. You're coming to our house. I insist. I'll go to the pharmacy and get you some Percocet for your pain. Barbara's got your room all ready to go."

ALONE IN HER ROOM IN THE KIRKLAND HOME, Anita thought about her relationship with Daryl. In those first months there were a few hints of his possessiveness and paranoia but nothing that Anita felt she couldn't handle. Once, she had phoned him from the hospital saying she thought she'd be home around 6:00 p.m. but was called to the ER to see an eighteen-month-old girl with a broken clavicle.

The x-rays on the child revealed that the toddler's clavicle was already healing in an awkward position and that it wasn't her first fracture. She also had a nasty diaper rash. The child appeared to be very frightened when her father entered the examination room. Suspecting that the father was neglectful and possibly abusive, she was required to call in Child Protective Services.

While attending to the child, Anita asked the nurse to make a quick call to Daryl and explain that she would be late coming home due to this situation in ER.

The nurse's lips were pursed in a stiff line when she returned. Quizzically, Anita asked if she reached him. "I called him but clearly he was annoyed and very abrupt with me. I was just delivering a message but he was very rude. He told me that this was the third time this month that you've been late and he hung up on me." She stared at Anita and shook her head.

"Oh, my gosh. I'm so sorry. I don't know why he would have acted like that. "

The nurse said, "Don't ask me to do that again," and she stormed down the corridor. Over her shoulder she said, "You got a live one there," rolling her eyes.

Daryl was clearly upset, stomping around the kitchen, when Anita got home at 9:00 p.m. She suspected he was drunk too.

"Daryl," she glared at him as she placed her keys on the kitchen counter. "How dare you treat one of my nurses so rudely?" He turned around toward the oven and pulled out an aluminum foil wrapped plate. "Here's your dinner," he said as he plunked it down on the granite counter top.

"Daryl, I'm a surgeon and I have an obligation to my patients. I was busy with a toddler who I believe was being abused by her father. I'm on call every third day, you know that. I had the nurse call you to tell you I would be late. Things happen that are out of my control. Please don't act like this." She walked over to him. "I wasn't trying to avoid you or be late. Things happen." She placed her hand on his arm.

He brushed her off.

"Daryl, you are being unreasonable." She stepped closer to him but he just stiffened his back.

"Maybe you just don't love me enough. I knew it

45

when you wouldn't take my last name when we got married. You didn't think our marriage would last."

"Daryl, we've discussed this so many times before we got married. I wanted to continue using my mother's name Stone. It's a little piece of her I'm holding onto. Why are you bringing this up now?

"You're too good to be a Davidson?"

"Stop. What are you talking about? This isn't about you or your last name. Come on, Daryl. You know I love you." She sighed deeply. "And, emergencies come up. We can still enjoy the rest of the evening together." She opened the cabinet to get a water glass. "What does being on call and attending to my patients have to do with my love for you?"

Instead of answering, she heard him tramping up the stairs. She was too tired and too hungry to argue with him any further. She had surgery at 7:00 a.m. She sat on the couch and blinked at the television, not paying attention just listening to the noise. Around 11:00 p.m. she went to bed.

In the morning Daryl was pleasant and very apologetic. She accepted his apology and thought the incident was resolved. However, after months of marriage the accusations escalated. Daryl was charming and understanding some times and accusatory and rude others. Anita couldn't figure out what set him off.

EIGHT

Anita opened her eyes, disoriented and confused. *Where am I?*

The room gradually lightened from its bleak cloudy gray hue to a golden yellow as her pupils adjusted to the room and reality set in. The throbbing pain from her fractured eye socket intensified. The heaviness of the cast on her right arm pulled her back to the events of the previous night. The Percocet made her woozy. Everything was still hazy. She dozed back to oblivion; a dream-like calm shrouded her thoughts of her third date with Daryl.

She tried on three different dresses before deciding on the butter-yellow sleeveless one, pulled tight at her waist, flaring at her hips. She thought it made her look more feminine than her actual tomboyish straight figure. In this dress she had curves. She covered her arms with a white cashmere sweater with pearl buttons. On her neck she wore the infinity diamond necklace with two interlocking circles that she had given her mother on the day her name, Anita Stone, M.D., was printed on the office door just below Thomas Kirkland, M.D. The necklace was hers now. She rarely took it off. Her wavy chestnut brown hair was free flowing to her shoulders. She hardly ever wore it down like that. Usually she pulled it in a ponytail high on her head out of her face so it could easily fit under a cap on surgery days.

ANITA SLOWLY OPENED THE FRONT DOOR. A SMILE pressed on her lips. Standing straight with his chest puffed out Daryl knocked on her front door. He was dressed in khaki pants and a starched, long-sleeved, ice-blue shirt opened at the collar. In his hands he held two dozen long-stemmed roses; one bunch was creamy lemonade-yellow, the other baby-lips pink.

"You look beautiful," Daryl said. He leaned over and gave her a kiss on the cheek. He offered up his bouquet-laden hands. "I couldn't decide which ones you would like so I bought them both. It looks like the yellow ones would have been the best choice to match your lovely dress."

"Thank you." She blushed. No one had bought

her flowers in a very long time. "What a sweet thing to do. Please come in." She bent her head down inhaling the sweet, honey scent of roses. "These smell wonderful. You didn't have to bring me flowers." She stepped away from the door and turned to go inside. "Follow me. Let me put these in water."

"It's my pleasure." He followed her down the hallway into the kitchen.

It was his first time here. The two-story house had high ceilings with an open loft overlooking the living room. The colors were beige and muted. The taupe leather furniture blended into the walls. There was a large painting of a sandy beach and palm above the couch.

Anita set the roses down on the kitchen counter and got two vases from the cabinets. She was filling them with water when Daryl found the kitchen scissors in the knife block on the counter and cut off the plastic wrapping around the flowers. He stood very close to Anita and touched her arms as he placed the roses in the vases. She fidgeted with the yellow blooms letting them splay out. She was aware of his closeness, his warmth, his musky, masculine smell.

"Is that all you have to do to them to make them look beautiful?" he asked.

Anita's lips turned upward in a smile. "They are already beautiful. I don't like to fuss with them much. Let them find their own place in the vase and in the crowd of the other buds." She stepped back to admire them. "They are ready."

"Well then, I can arrange the pink ones," Daryl said. His strong hands looked awkward around the thin, straight thornless stems but he wiggled them and smiled. "I think they found their places in the crowd."

"Looks perfect to me. Thank you again."

Daryl leaned over and gave Anita a whisper kiss on the cheek. Anita inhaled a sweet scent of vanilla mingled with the roses. "Shall we go? I have reservations but it will take us a while to get to the restaurant," Daryl said.

"I'm ready. Where are we going?"

"It's a surprise." He grinned and took the back of her elbow escorting her outside. At the street he opened the passenger door of his carmine red Porsche and let her settle into the rich leather seat. She looked up at him. "Quite the gentleman."

"Always," he replied as he leaned over to kiss her cheek for the second time in minutes. He walked around the car, got into the driver's seat and looked over at her. "Yellow is so beautiful with your skin. Are you ready for a ride?"

"Sure," she grinned, wondering if she was going to get more than one ride tonight; one in the car and one in her bed.

Daryl had arranged for a private table at a small bistro in San Francisco. A bottle of chilled French champagne was in a silver bucket awaiting their arrival. They dined on romaine and pear salad, butternut squash ravioli and lobster. Daryl ordered a glass of Rombauer Chardonnay to pair with the lobster. For dessert he ordered one slice of chocolate decadence cake which they shared, Daryl teasingly feeding her. They topped off the evening with a glass of Sauterne, a sweet French wine. Their conversation flowed as easily as the wine. Mellow.

After a very romantic, candlelit dinner Daryl brought them back to her house. She was feeling light-headed, sexy and amorous. Daryl had been the perfect gentlemen that evening.

Finally, she thought, a man not intimidated by the M.D. after my name. He took charge when ordering the dinner, paired the meal with top-of-the-line wines and ordered only one dessert. *How sexy was that? I wonder how much he takes charge in the bedroom.*

When the two of them returned to Anita's house, she coyly led Daryl by the hand up the stairs to her bedroom. She turned the stereo to soft jazz. Daryl was standing close to her. Teasingly, she gently pushed him onto her milky-white duvet. She reached over her shoulder to undo the zipper of her dress.

"Turn around," Daryl said in his low masculine voice as he raised on his elbows. "Let me do that. I want to undress you. I want to savor this night."

Anita turned around and let Daryl take control. She was ripe with desire. He stood up from the bed behind her and expertly undressed her, kissing her neck and back. Daryl watched her shiver with anticipation but took his time disrobing her, kissing her back, letting her dress pool around her ankles. She kicked the dress off to the side and turned around.

His gaze went to her small, smooth breasts. He caressed them with his hands, then his tongue. She wrapped her arms around him pulling him in close. She was ready for him. She wanted his clothes off. She tugged at his shirt. It was too tight to pull over his head so he stepped back.

"Patience, my dear. I want to relish your body. It's so perfect, so soft, so inviting." He took off his shirt and tossed it on the chair by the window. She drew him to her, feeling the warmth of his chest on her bare breasts.

"You feel so good." she whispered. "I want you." She nibbled at his ear inhaling his manly scent. "I want you. All of you." Anita nuzzled her head into his neck.

She undid his belt. Then Daryl took over, unbuttoning his pants and letting them fall to the carpet. His full erection was tugging his underwear tight. He pulled them down. She reached for his penis and held it in her hands; warm and hard. "I want this. I want this inside of me," she panted. She melted down on the bed and pulled him on top of her. She was ready. With her fingers clenched around his muscular backside, he entered her slowly. Then, he moved in perfect synch to the jazz on the radio. She drew him in, drowning in his smell. Anita's heart raced with anticipation. She craved more. She wanted a release. He thrust his manhood into her without restraint. She couldn't get enough, pulling him tighter to her silky-wet flesh.

"More, more," she murmured. And, she got more. More of his manhood. More of his thrusts. With abandon she climaxed. "Yes, yes," she mumbled. Then he climaxed.

Sated, their bodies dissolved into oblivion, exhausted and spent. Wrapped in each other's arms they fell into a deep sleep.

A muted glow from the windows awakened her. It was dawn. The bed was empty. Daryl was gone. She smelled the faint coconut scent of her shampoo lofting from her bathroom and heard a quiet drip from the shower. Daryl must have taken a shower and left while she was still sleeping. On his pillow was a pink envelope from her stationary collection downstairs. Anita found it interesting that he would use her pink stationary instead of her plain white note paper. She noted her name in blocked, masculine, all capital letters, a sharp contrast to the muted pink envelope. She reached for it. Roses perfumed the room reminding her of the two dozen Daryl had brought the previous night. The yellow ones were now on her dresser.

Anita slipped her finger under the flap of the envelope and pulled out a piece of her stationary. She wasn't ready for the day to begin; wasn't ready for their night to be over. The note said,

Darling Anita,

Our evening was the best I've had in years. I can still taste the sweetness of your lips on my mouth. My skin still tingles

from your touch. I did not want to wake you. Sweet dreams my lady. I'll be back.

XXOO

Daryl

Anita put the note down and picked up the pillow Daryl had slept on. The pillow was cool to her cheek. She pressed it close to her chest, burying her face in its musky fragrance. She inhaled deeply and remembered how he smelled last night.

A PILLOW ENVELOPED HER CHEEK AS SHE STIRRED. She was in the tidy, spare bedroom at Thomas's and Barbara's house. The down comforter softly rubbed her aching chin. A light streamed under the door sill. Anita gingerly sat up, a little dizzy at first.

How long have I been asleep? What time is it?

She scanned the room for a clock finding one on the nightstand. It was 10:02. *I haven't slept in until ten o'clock in the morning since when ... high school. Oh my god. I've got to get going.* Her dizzy mind flashed with random thoughts. *Wait. Where am I going? It's Saturday. The office is closed. I'm not going anywhere right now. I feel awful, like I've been hit and dragged down the pavement under a semi.*

Gingerly she rolled over and inched back down under the covers not yet ready to face the world. Faintly, she heard Thomas and Barbara talking from somewhere in the house. Her fuzzy mind wasn't ready, too tousled for company. With a full bladder she quietly shuffled down the hallway to the bathroom. When she switched on the light, a battered reflection of Anita stared back at her from the mirror, startling her. She could barely open her swollen, plum and black left eye. Her chin was puffy and blue. Her long hair, disheveled and matted, framed her lopsided and distorted face.

"I look like a train hit me. How pathetic. He really hit me hard this time." She slowly returned back to the bedroom and gently closed the door. Sitting delicately down on the bed, she noticed a photo atop a crocheted doily on the nightstand. It was a picture of the backs of a couple holding hands peering into the shimmering crystal blue ocean. Their feet were blanketed in golden sand and the emerald fronds of the palm trees to the right of the couple were bent slightly toward them. *Thomas and Barbara probably on one of their many trips to Maui. What a peaceful picture.* Although their faces were hidden, she could sense their bond by the way they stood, leaning toward each other.

"Oh, that's what love is supposed to look like," she murmured.

There was a gentle tap on the door. "Anita, I've brought you a cup of tea. May I come in?"

"Yes, Barbara. I'd love a cup of tea but before you open the door I have to warn you, I'm not going to win any beauty contests this morning. Maybe you should put on some dark glasses before you enter. Or better yet, do you have a couple pair of rose-colored ones? I think we're both going to need them."

Grinning at Anita's sense of humor even during this difficult situation, Barbara opened the door carrying a cup of tea.

Barbara was alarmed at Anita's puffy and battered face yet careful not to reveal her concern in her tone of voice—a trick she had learned from her husband. "Yes, young lady. I'm not voting for you in this morning's beauty pageant but, there's still hope. I wonder how you'll do in the talent contest." She smiled.

"I don't think I'll do well with that contest either. I was planning on singing, "Put on a Happy Face." Anita smiled at her own joke.

"You're too much. Don't make me laugh so hard. I'll spill the hot tea on you and you'll end up back in the ER."

They both chuckled, nervous, edgy giggles.

Barbara set the tea on the bedside table and sat on the bed next to Anita. Cautiously, she said, "You look pretty rough. Truthfully, it makes me mad to see you like this, to know that Daryl did this to you. Andy assured us that he'd keep a close watch on your eye. He said he'd know more once the swelling goes down and the fractures heal. Do you see okay?"

"Well, it depends on what I'm looking at. Right now, I don't see my future very clearly, but I don't have double vision if that's what you mean. That's what Andy told me to watch out for."

"That's what I meant." There was a long pause.

"How are you feeling?"

"About as good as I look. The Percocet has almost worn off. I'm ready for another one."

Barbara stood, "I'll get you one. They are in the kitchen. I'm going to bring you some scrambled eggs and toast with my famous homemade apricot jam so you don't take it on an empty stomach."

"You don't have to do that."

"Yes, I do. I'll be right back."

ANITA SWALLOWED HER PERCOCET AND ATE EVERY bite of her fluffy scrambled eggs and toast while Barbara silently sat on the antique chair next to the bed, sipping her tea. When Anita was finished, Barbara took the tray of food and set it on the dresser.

"Barbara, may I ask you a question?"

"Of course."

"In this picture on the nightstand of you and Thomas, you appear to be so close, so connected. So in love. Has it always been that way for the two of you?"

"Mostly, yes. Of course, there were some hard times, but our love was always strong. We went through a rough patch when I found out I couldn't have children. We had dreamt of having a large family. It was difficult for both of us but neither of us ever considered leaving the marriage. We have always loved each other, supported each other, if that's what you mean. Thomas is the one who convinced me to go back and get my master's degree so I could become a principal. That's what love is, Anita— encouraging each other to be the best they can be. And, I know with certainty that Thomas would never do anything to hurt me. Love should not hurt." Continuing with a firmer pitch in her voice, "Nothing about a balled up fist to the eye is love. What you have with Daryl isn't love at all, its abuse."

"He wasn't always mean, Barbara."

"Really?" Raising her voice again, Barbara said, "But, Anita, if he can do this to you at any time, he doesn't really love you. He's got some major issues. I've seen it in some of my high school kids that bully others. It starts very young. No one should ever even consider hitting anyone. It's hard for me to see you defending him. "

Shaking her head, "No … no, I'm not defending him."

"Yes, you are, Anita." Barbara stared, razor focused toward Anita. "What he's done to you is a crime, and Thomas and I can't sit back and ignore it any longer. We can't watch you get beat up again. We suspected something was wrong for some time. We both thought we saw bruising on your face and then there was the way you avoided us. We should have spoken up, tried to help earlier. I don't care that Daryl isn't always mean to you or that you think you loved him or he apologizes again. Thomas and I can't watch this anymore." Her voice was shaking and loud.

Anita's face was solemn. "I thought I had covered it up."

"No, we knew, or at least strongly suspected, but we thought or hoped you would come to us if you needed help. What you have with Daryl isn't love, Anita."

Anita uttered. "I just don't understand. There's so much I don't understand. Why would he say he loves me then hurt me, punch me and try to control me?" She shook her head.

"That's typical of abusers, bullies."

"Barbara, nothing prepared me for this. I don't know what to do. What do I do next?"

Getting up from her chair and gently putting her arm around Anita's shoulder, Barbara assured Anita, "Rest and get well. Thomas and I will help you through this."

Leaning her head down, Anita muttered, "Barbara, I feel so stupid. How could I have gotten into this mess?"

"Anita, you are anything but stupid. Just because you got into this bad relationship doesn't discount all that you have accomplished in your life. Thomas and I are so proud of you. You're an intelligent, compassionate, beautiful woman and a respected doctor. Your relationship with Daryl does not define you or take away from anything you're done or who you are. You'll get through this. I promise. There is a light at the end of this tunnel. Right now, you should rest and heal."

"I don't have any clothes. I don't have my car. I don't know what's happened to Daryl or where he is." Anita cast her eyes down.

"Just rest, Anita. Please don't fret. There is nothing to worry about right now. You are safe and warm and in a loving house. You need to let your body heal. I promise you we'll figure all this out in the next few days." She took another look at the picture on the nightstand. "That's love Anita. After nearly four decades, that's true love. You will get out of this and find it too."

Anita pulled the soft down comforter up to her bruised chin as she relaxed into the combination of Percocet and Barbara's reassuring words. She leaned back on the pillows feeling a wave of sleepiness envelope her. "Thank you, Barbara. I'd like to rest a bit now. I love you."

"I love you too." Barbara leaned down and kissed Anita's clammy forehead. Quietly, Barbara turned, tiptoed out of the room and quietly shut the door, leaving Anita to heal.

NINE

DARYL'S FRIDAY NIGHT WAS VERY DIFFERENT than Anita's. Stunned by Anita's punch and dash down the stairs, he darted down the stairs two at a time and into the entryway after her. The front door was wide open. She was gone. He bolted out onto the sidewalk but it was too dark to see.

"Anita, where are you?" Daryl shouted. I know you're out here. Answer me. Where are you?"

He didn't hear an answer. He turned his head listening, searching. Silence.

Turning back toward the house, he muttered to himself, "Damn bitch. How dare you ruin my Friday night? We were supposed to be celebrating my big deal. You shouldn't have left the dinner table when I was just getting romantic. How dare you dismiss me? Again, you asked for what you got. I need to be fucked, goddamn it. I'm your husband for Christ's sakes. You can't deny me. I know I'm not some high, prestigious doctor and I don't save lives," he said sarcastically, "but, I make a decent living, take you to the nicest restaurants, and buy you flowers and jewelry." He continued his rambling to himself, "I'm a top salesman. Your prissy doctor friends don't have to go out and sell every day. I work hard, damn it. I deserve some respect. Now I have to go find you. This isn't how I was planning on spending my Friday night."

He stomped into the kitchen, searching, rummaging around for his keys. He saw his Porsche key lying on the kitchen counter. She had his key ring with all the other keys.

"That's right. I remember now. You took my whole damn key ring this morning leaving me only the Porsche key when you were running late and couldn't find your own keys. Damn bitch." He yanked the key off the counter and hurried into the garage.

He backed out revving the engine of his Porsche. Slowly he drove down the street hunting for her. Impatiently scanning both sides of the street as he drove, he muttered, "Where'd she go? She couldn't be very far."

He drove down Adams Circle and out the only neighborhood entrance to their housing complex onto Washington Street. He didn't see her. He didn't see anybody on the sidewalks. He drove around slowing hunting for her. Convinced that she would just come home soon, or was possibly back by now, he made a U-turn and headed back home. When he got inside, he scanned the downstairs. She wasn't there. He ran up the stairs. Not there either. She wasn't home.

Frustrated, he poured himself a Scotch and soda and gulped the whole drink. He slammed the empty glass down on the granite counter. Snarling, he said, "Ok, if that's how you want it to be, I'll just let you stay out in the cold, you selfish bitchy ass."

He poured himself another drink and took it into the family room, plopped down on the leather sofa and turned on the television. Flipping through the channels, he kept one ear alert to the front door, expecting Anita to come back at any time. When he realized his drink was gone and she still wasn't home, he staggered back into the kitchen and made himself another Scotch. "A night cap. That's what will settle my nerves. Damn bitch, if she wants to be out all night in the cold, so be it. I'm enjoying my drink and going to bed."

Haltingly, he stumbled up the stairs; his feet heavy, feeling like he had on cement-filled rubber boots. He gripped the railing, stopping every few steps to steady his swaying body and stop the stairs from spinning. At each resting step, he took another sip of his drink.

Once upstairs, he staggered down the hallway bumping into the partially open master bedroom door.

"Leave me alone, door. I've had a rough night."
He hit the door with his shoulder. It bounced back.
"Damn door."

Clumsily, he set his nightcap on the night stand.
The room spun around. He swayed on his feet,
snickering to himself until he finally fell down on the
bed. Fumbling, he finally got his pants off. His drink
spilled all over him as he reached for one last sip.

"Damn, it. Damn bitch," he garbled as he
clumsily wiped the Scotch off himself. He passed out
on top of the covers.

Sometime in the night, Daryl thought he heard
someone banging on the door, but in his muddled
drunken stupor he couldn't decide where the
pounding was coming from. *Is it real or is it a dream, the
same recurring dream from my childhood? Is she home?*

FROM THE TIME HE WAS EIGHT YEARS OLD HE WOKE
often from his persistent dream. Back then, he
couldn't tell if he was dreaming or awake when he
heard the knocks on the front door. He'd sleepwalk,
his bare feet skimming the worn carpeting as he raced
to the door hoping his mother was there. She never
was.

TEN

DARYL DELVED INTO HIS CHILDHOOD. THE LAST few months, Mom has been difficult to live with. She wasn't always like this. We used to have happy talks at the dinner table. Now she snaps at the slightest irritation. She's always scolded Dad, yelling at him for his forgetfulness or lack of paying attention to her.

Dad took it, every mean thing she said to him. He didn't respond, didn't flinch, didn't counterattack, didn't say a word—just shrugged his shoulders. He went about his usual business at the end of his work day; first opening his steel domed lunchbox, opening his Thermos and rinsing out the last of his cold coffee, placing it on a towel to dry, putting his empty lunchbox in the cupboard and, finally, heading for the bathroom to shower and change for dinner.

At around thirteen, my sister, Mattie, changed

into a mini-mom. She yelled at me to turn down the television, stomped around the house, made fun of my friends, made snarky remarks to me all the time.

On one Friday, as usual, Mattie was waiting for me at the playground by my elementary school. In her sassy voice she said, "Daryl, why are you always … like … the last one out of your class? Can't you get out of there faster? I have better things to do than wait around for my punk little brother. Come on. Let's go." She dragged me by my arm. We walked home past abandoned cars parked on what used to be green lawns. Sickly brown weeds decorated their tires. I played the game of not stepping on any cracks (*Step on a crack, you'll break your mother's back*) as we walked home. Mattie pushed me trying to make me step on a crack and then laughed when I did.

When we got home, we threw our books on the creaky, pine kitchen table. Mom's car was gone which was weird since she was always home, usually sitting on the couch with her eyes glued to her soap opera.

"Where's Mom?" I asked her.

"How should I know, dummy?" She snarled her lips. "You're such a weirdo. You're a bugger head."

"No I'm not. You are."

"She must have gone to the store. I don't know," Mattie told me. "We better get our homework started before she comes home and gets mad at us."

Mattie poured each of us a small glass of cold milk and got cookies out of the pine cupboard above the stove. Mom let us each have three paper-thin cookie-wafers before we started our homework. They came in three different colors and flavors—pink was strawberry, white was vanilla and brown was chocolate. Pink was my least favorite. What I would have done to have an Oreo cookie, but Oreos were way too expensive. That's what Mom always said when Mattie and I begged for them.

Oh … Oreos. Sometimes Johnny, my best friend, let me trade my three wafer cookies for one Oreo. I went into a trance, twisting the dark colored cookie apart revealing the creamy, rich, white insides. I'd slowly lick the white frosting layer side. When the crisp chocolate cookie part started to dissolve on my tongue, I stuffed the rest of the crunchy cookie in my mouth. Oreos, my favorite cookies.

Since Mom always insisted we do our homework right after school, "before we got distracted," she said, I sat down to work on mine. I opened my math book and stared at the numbers on the page scratching my head. "Mattie, I don't know how to do this problem. Can you help me?"

"Daryl, why? It's so simple. Are you that stupid or what?"

I sneered at her, "No, I'm not stupid. Don't call me that. You're acting just like Mom when she's mad."

"No, I'm not."

"Yes, you are. Leave me alone. I wish I had never asked you." Boldly, I turned my chair around so I wouldn't have to see my sister's buggy snarls.

I quickly finished the homework I could do and slammed my book closed. "I'm done for now. Mom will help me when she gets home. I'm going in the backyard to find some lizards. Maybe I'll ask Mom to cook them up for your dinner. Neener … neener."

"You're just a punk kid. Bet you can't even catch a lizard."

"Yes I can. You'll see." I yanked the sliding glass door shut with all my might. The plate glass door vibrated in my small hand.

An hour later, tired and bored of my hunt for lizards, I came back into the kitchen. Mattie was still at the round kitchen table, her long straight blond hair falling in front of her face as she leaned over her textbook.

"Mom home yet?"

Mattie turned her head around and glared at me. She peered around the room. "Do you see her? No, she's not home. Duh."

In my shaky voice I asked, "Where is she?"

"Do I look like I know?" She turned back to her book. "I have to finish my homework. Mom will be home soon."

But she wasn't.

Dad got home from work reeking of grease and oil. He started his normal routine of rinsing out his metal Thermos. I popped up from the couch. "Dad, where's Mom?"

"I don't know. Did she leave a note?"

I shook my head. "We didn't see one."

68

Mattie chimed in from the family room, above the noise of cartoons. "No, she wasn't here when we got home from school."

Dad looked puzzled. "She wasn't?"

"No ... we didn't see anything."

Dad left his lunchbox on the tile counter and walked around the corner and into their bedroom. On top of the dusty black, pressed-board dresser Dad found a white envelope with his name, Frank, written on the outside.

Dad came out of the bedroom ghost-white and my life turned upside down. Mattie and I, seated on the rundown, ragged couch, watched as my ashen-faced father came around the hallway with a crumpled piece of paper in his hand. Alarmed at his appearance Mattie jumped up and asked, "What happened? Dad, what's going on?"

Dad didn't answer. He didn't look at us. It was as if we weren't there ... ghosts. His eyes were damp. He sank into the opposite side of the old couch and stared forward, shaking his head. I didn't know what to do. Mattie sat down next to me and gently placed her hand in mine. She scanned Dad's drawn face for answers. Pasty white with his head bent forward, he patted the empty area next to him on the couch, coaxing us, as he would our dog, to come sit next to him. I scooted near my dad; Mattie next to me. Slowly, he turned his head toward us. With glistening eyes he said. "Mom has left. She packed her bags and left. Just like that. She left this note." He showed us the wadded up, wrinkled paper in his hand. "She's not happy anymore. She said she'd call us later during the week after she sorts out some things."

My mind went boggy. The wax in my ears buzzed. I was confused. I stared at Mattie's face. She was crying. Fiercely I searched my dad's flecked hazel eyes for answers. *I can't be hearing this right. Is he talking about my mom? What does he mean she packed and left? She isn't happy? What did we do? Moms don't just pack their bags and leave. What is he talking about?*

"Dad, what do you mean she left? Where did she go? When will she be home?"

"I don't know, Daryl. I don't know." His straight-lipped expression and wet eyes said it all. I snuggled into my dad's chest and quietly whimpered. Mattie scooted closer and bent her head down.

Sometime that weekend, Dad showed Mattie the hand written note. Mattie told me what it said. She had memorized it.

Frank,

You don't pay any attention to me anymore. You don't give me credit for all that I have done taking care of the house and the kids. It's like we're strangers and I'm not happy anymore. I am leaving you for someone who cares about me and makes me happy. You can take care of the house and kids for now and see how hard it has been on me. I've contacted an attorney for a divorce. I will call the kids and explain next week.

Bye, Jill

I cried the rest of the weekend and stayed in bed thinking if I had only been better at math, or if I had made my bed when she asked me to, or picked up my toys, or hadn't made such a fuss about not liking broccoli, then Mom would have stayed. I would tell her when she called that I'd be good and study harder. She would come back.

But … Mom didn't come back. She moved to the other side of town with this guy named Robert. She picked me up on Wednesdays, and we went to this stranger's house where Mom now lived. She made my favorite meals; spaghetti, tacos or macaroni and cheese with peas. I pretended to be having fun but I wanted Mom to come home. I didn't like Robert. He didn't do anything bad, but I wanted my dad and my mom to live together again. I went with her on every other weekend too. She picked me up at my dad's house. It was very strange having my mom honk in the driveway for me to come out and get in her car. Nothing seemed right. Dad didn't want to talk to her, neither did Mattie, but I wanted my mom. I tried for months to talk her into coming back. I told her how much I had been studying and how neat my room was, but Mom kept telling me it wasn't about me. She said she loved me and always would.

Mattie rarely came with me on Wednesdays, sometimes on the weekends. She was very angry at Mom.

Teenage Mattie became a grown-up overnight. She had to learn to cook and take care of the house and take care of me too. I tried to help and even did my own laundry, but she was constantly yelling and stomping around the house. I tried to talk to Mom about it, but she said it was just a phase. I begged to go live with Mom but Dad didn't like the idea—wouldn't allow it. Mom didn't think it was a good idea either.

After Mom moved out I noticed her saying some strange things about neighbors watching her and having to keep her curtains closed during the day. She talked about spies and detectives that were after her. None of this made sense to me. Nothing made sense to me anymore. Then, Mom started spending our weekends in bed sleeping. I was lost and alone.

"Mom, you need to get up," I begged one day before dinner. "It's only 6:00 o'clock. Why are you in bed now?"

Her drapes were pulled shut. Covers tucked mummy-like around her thinning body. "I'm tired. I need my rest," she said. "Leave me alone. Go play or something. Turn on the TV. You're old enough to entertain yourself now."

This was a typical conversation at Mom's house.

Dad mostly ignored Mattie and me. He went to work every day before I got out of bed. "I have to work. That's how we eat and have a roof over our heads." When he got home, as long as there was dinner on the table and our homework done, he thought things were okay. They weren't. I still did all my homework and got good grades, but Mom didn't come back to live with us.

Then, one Wednesday Mom didn't show up to pick me up. Robert called and said she was in the hospital and would be there for a long time. He said she had a nervous breakdown, whatever that meant. Nobody would let me see her while she was in the hospital.

It was years before I saw Mom again. I was a teenager. She wasn't the same. Her voice was flat, her eyes dazed, her face expressionless. She didn't pick me up from Dad's anymore. Occasionally, she and Robert would come by in the summer and we'd go get an ice cream at the park, but Mom barely spoke during our visits. She gazed out at the duck pond and watched the ducks float around. Robert brought bread for her to feed them. She spoke to them in a soft, motherly, quiet voice as if, now, they were her children, her babies. It was very odd hanging out with Mom and Robert. At least Robert played catch with me now but mom just sat and watched. The visits were very uncomfortable.

Mattie and I drifted through life without direction … without affection. At eighteen Mattie got pregnant and went to live with her boyfriend's family. I had just turned thirteen.

ELEVEN

SATURDAY WAS A BLUR FOR ANITA. AS SHE DRIFTED in and out of sleep, her thoughts ping-ponging between the charming, sexy Daryl and the aggressive, mean one.

Daryl had wooed her with his charm, charisma, sense of humor, romantic getaways, and inventive, skillful sex. He was worldly and knew about food and wine. She accompanied him to a sales conference in Seattle where she was introduced to his fellow workers. Life was thrilling again. She felt desired, adored and sexy. Daryl wanted to be with her all the time, and after a few months of dating he was basically living at her house. He stopped by her office with yellow roses at least twice a month and whisked her away during her lunch hour. Sometimes they ate during their rendezvous but usually not. Usually they drove home and made love.

THE OTHER DARYL THREW VERBAL JABS AND PUT downs. Although Anita could rationalize those away, they still hurt deeply. *Why did Daryl tell her she was stupid when she was a board certified orthopedic surgeon? It didn't make sense. Of course, it didn't make sense. He wasn't rational when he drank. The liquor made him a monster. Was it just the liquor?* They had been married just over a year when the physical beatings started and when they did, they escalated in frequency and severity each successive time.

There were the apologies in the mornings, and she believed him at first, but then the cycle would start again on another night after just a few drinks.

Six months ago he broke her left ulna. His rationale was that Anita provoked him when she refused to drink the glass of champagne he had brought upstairs for her. It was 1:00 a.m. and she was sound asleep when he brought up the drink. She tried to reason with him and walk away, go downstairs, but he caught up with her. She had to have her arm X-rayed and cast. She told the ER doctor that she slipped and fell over a shoe on the stairs.

She could still practice medicine in a cast and do most of her surgeries. Humiliated, she lied to the staff about how it happened. Deep, suppressed feelings of not being good enough, especially for her dad, surfaced. She didn't want to get divorced again. She asked Daryl to go to counseling with her.

He went twice saying he was deeply sorry and it wouldn't happen again. He charmed even the counselor into believing him, but after a few months of calm, the abuse started again. First it was drunken slurred put-downs which Anita tried to ignore. Then it became physical. When he started hitting her with his fists, she went back to the counselor. Daryl refused to go, dismissing his behavior, saying she prompted his violence but each time promising it wouldn't happen again. Anita realized she needed to take action to get away from Daryl but deep seeded insecurities surfaced. She resisted the plan the counselor and she made. She still hoped Daryl would change back to the man she dated, the one who whisked her off to a Bed and Breakfast in Capitola mid-day for love making after drinking champagne in wine flutes on the beach, the one who woke early and snuck out of bed to whip up her favorite eggs Florentine before her busy day in the OR. The one who charmed her and wooed her, rubbed her aching feet at night and left romantic notes all over the house. That's the Daryl she wanted back. That's the Daryl she didn't want to give up. Not the strong-armed Daryl with the violent temper and closed fists.

BY SUNDAY MORNING HER THOUGHTS TURNED more to the present and she was feeling well enough to face the world, or at least Thomas and Barbara. She dressed in the casual sweats Barbara had laid out for her, brushed her tangled, matted hair, and awkwardly made her way down the hallway, creeping like an old worn-down woman, her upper body still feeling like a truck ran over it. She was drawn to the kitchen by the aroma of freshly baked muffins.

"Good morning, Sunshine," Barbara said. Her hair was perfectly styled and her eyes were as bright as headlamps. She stood and wrapped her motherly arms around Anita.

"I'm not sure the sun is shining all that brightly but good morning to you too." Anita gave Barbara a gentle hug then made her way to Thomas who was sitting with his reading glasses propped on his nose, a warm smile on his face, and the Sunday paper opened to the sports section.

"Good morning, Thomas." She gave him a tender tap on his shoulder.

He reached his steady hand to hers and lovingly patted it. She felt the weight of his hand, reassuring and protective. "How are you, my dear?" he said in his cocoa-smooth baritone.

"I'm okay. I've been better, but I'm so grateful to you and . . ." glancing up, "and Barbara, of course."

"Come enjoy a cup of tea. Barbara makes the most amazing cranberry zucchini muffins. She only makes them for me on special occasions. This must be one of them."

"Thank you. Hot tea and muffins sound delightful." Anita sat opposite Thomas while Barbara put on the tea kettle. Glancing across at Thomas, she said, "This is a nightmare, Thomas. I'm so sorry you're involved."

"Nonsense. We should have gotten involved earlier."

With her uninjured eye downcast, the other one now swollen shut she murmured, "I was too ashamed to tell anybody, even you two. I thought I could handle this by myself. I kept thinking it was the last time and things would get better." Anita shifted in her chair. "But, you knew something was going on, didn't you?"

"Yes, I wish we had done or said something when we suspected. There was the time you came into the office a couple of months ago with what appeared to be a bruise on your cheek. I wondered then but didn't say anything."

Anita remembered that specific argument and fight.

IT WAS A FRIDAY NIGHT. DARYL HAD INVITED TWO co-workers to join them for dinner in San Francisco after closing a big sale at Children's Hospital. It was time to celebrate. Anita was thrilled for Daryl and his co-workers and excited to let her hair down too, after a very long week of complicated surgeries.

That was one of the things she most loved about Daryl. He knew how to celebrate with abandon and put cares and worries on the sideline; tuck work neatly away in his back pocket until Monday. Anita wasn't very good at that but Thomas was on call for the week-end.

Daryl and Anita met Michael and Lawrence at Tadich Grill on California Street in the City. Daryl wanted to show Anita off to his co-workers even though the other wives could not make it. This third oldest restaurant in America was crowded and loud with suit-clad business men. The huge mahogany bar, which extended all the way from front to back of the restaurant, didn't have an empty seat. As Anita entered the restaurant, she noted a slight hint of long past cigar smoke which seeped into her lungs permeating through the walls from patrons of yesteryear. The three men crowded around other patrons cajoling and drinking scotch at the end of the bar. Anita wasn't into hard liquor. Instead, she sipped on her normal glass of Rombauer chardonnay.

After a few drinks the four of them were seated for dinner. Each ordered the famous Seafood Cioppino with garlic bread. The mood was enthusiastic and lively with lots of hand shaking and slaps on the back; this in direct contrast with the formal attire of white jackets and black pants of the waiters.

The messy dish contributed to their mood as they cracked the crab legs in their sauce-covered dripping hands and threw the discarded shells in a bowl in the middle of the table. This became a competition with whoops and hollers as each shell made it into the bowl. Anita determined that she would be the one driving home as Daryl's drinking continued.

Around midnight, after saying good-bye to their friends, Anita and Daryl walked in the opposite direction to their car. She quietly asked Daryl for his keys.

"I'm fine to drive," Daryl answered. He shoved his hands deeper into his pockets. "I'm not a wimp. I can hold my alcohol."

Anita stopped on the sidewalk and glared at him. "I'm not kidding, Daryl. You've had too much to drink to drive. Just give me the keys." She reached out her hand.

"No way. I'm driving my Porsche home. You barely know how to drive it and I certainly won't let you drive in the City." He shook his head back and forth and continued stomping down the street.

When they reached the car, Daryl stumbled down the curb before righting himself and puffing out his chest like he had just won a championship boxing match instead of drunk-stumbling down a curb. Anita stood firm, glowering at him. "You are not driving us home."

"That's ridiculous," he slurred as he opened the driver's door.

"I'm not getting in the car with you. You should not be driving." Anita lifted her hand and made a stopping gesture.

Daryl got in the car and defiantly slammed the door closed.

Anita opened the passenger-side door and leaned in. Her voice was steady. "I'm not getting in the car.

This is ridiculous. Daryl, come on. Let me drive us home. I've had only two glasses of wine. I'm fine to drive." Her voice grew softer, sounding as if she was trying to coax a baby cotton-tail out from the bushes. "Please. It's no big deal. Come on."

"Get in, Babe. I'm fine."

"No," she said. Her voice was firm yet smooth.

"Ha."

"Let me drive home." Anita thought about walking away. Instead, she gently shook her head while leaning into the car. "I'm not getting in. You shouldn't drive in your condition. Daryl, I'm being serious." She slowed and calmed her words as if she were talking to an upset toddler. "Please just get out and let me drive. There are no big hills on our way to the freeway. I'll be fine."

Daryl stared at her full on. "You're so prissy." His lips snarled.

"If that's what you want to call me." She inhaled. "But, I'm not getting into the passenger seat." She stood firm.

Finally Daryl acquiesced. Clumsily, he got out of the driver's seat leaving the keys in the ignition. He stutter-stepped over to the passenger side of the car then awkwardly flopped into the seat and slammed the door. Anita marched around the car and got in.

The ride home was eerily quiet but when they got into the house Daryl let out a rant of swear words. He accused Anita of embarrassing him in front of his co-workers even though they had already left.

Anita put the keys on the entry-way table and walked upstairs. Daryl followed closely behind her. When they got to the top of the stairs, Daryl grabbed Anita around her shoulders, twisting her toward him. His breath reeked of alcohol. "Don't ever question my judgment. I know when I can drive and when I can't." His thick-tongued words were heavy. His icy tone made her flinch with fear.

"You're hurting me. Let me go. Daryl. Stop this." She tried to escape his grip. He slapped her across the face jerking her head back. Then, he shoved her backwards into the wall behind her.

"Daryl, stop this. What are you doing? You need to go to bed. Leave me alone."

"Cunt," he shouted. He lurched into the bedroom and flopped on the top of the bed.

Anita went into the hallway bathroom and checked out the red marks on her face. She paused as she saw her reflection in the mirror. *What is happening here? Daryl just hit me.* She washed the marks on her cheeks with cold water. There was an ashen taste in her mouth. She had trouble swallowing the thick, sour taste of fear. The room seemed to shrink around her.

She peered into the bedroom. Daryl had not moved. His legs sprawled spread eagle on the bed. She left him there, pulled out a pillow and blanket from the hall closet, and quietly descended downstairs. *What just happened?*

She collapsed onto the leather couch, pulled the blanket over her head and sobbed. Lead-filled anxiety oozed into the pit of her stomach.

IN THE MORNING DARYL WAS EXTREMELY apologetic. He assured her nothing like that would ever happen again. He said he didn't know what had gotten into him.

Anita didn't know what to think; unable to process the yin and yang of her swirling thoughts. She loved this man but she didn't like him last night. She was afraid of him.

THE LOUD WHISTLING TEA KETTLE MADE ANITA temporarily freeze. Her shoulders tensed with the noise but eased when Barbara took the kettle off the stove. Barbara handed Anita a cup of tea. The muffins, displayed on an ornamental serving dish, sat in the center of the table, a crystal bowl of cut fruit beside it. There was combined silence; Anita and the Kirklands eating muffins and sipping tea. No one spoke until Thomas finished an article in the paper. He took off his glasses and gazed toward Anita.

"Anita, Barbara and I would like you to spend some time at our Pajaro Dunes beach house. Barbara has wanted to go for weeks now. We think the sunshine, salt air, and ocean breezes will be good for you. I'll handle the practice for a while. Yesterday I spoke with John Osborn, a good friend and a family law attorney. He advised me that you should get an emergency restraining order."

"Thomas, I … I … don't know about a restraining order. I …" Unconsciously, she crumbled the muffin in her damp hands. Interrupting her, Thomas asked, "Will you seriously consider it? He advised it and I think it is in your best interest."

"Let me think." She folded her hands around the warm, bone china tea cup and stared into it as if it would give her the answers she was looking for. "Thomas, I'll go to the beach house. I don't want to be around town looking like this. I don't want to accidently run into a patient or Daryl. Thank you so much for taking over my case load."

"You don't have to worry about your patients."

"I know." She kicked into efficient doctor mode. "I have a couple surgeries planned Tuesday. They are straight forward though, a knee arthroscopy and meniscectomy on a 60-year-old man and a carpal tunnel release on a 54-year-old female. Neither of them have heart or health issues. Pretty routine. I'm sure Susan will explain my absence to them and my other patients. She is so good at that. They will be okay with you doing their surgeries." Anita's head started pounding. "I've got to call Susan and ask her to come in early Monday."

"Anita, the practice isn't what you should be worried about. I'll take care of it until you're back in shape. You need to focus on the other aspects of your life, especially being safe. Please, let us help you."

Anita's heart rate increased, her body flooded warm, anxiety taking over. She fidgeted with her napkin. Her mind was spinning again like a child's toy top. "I don't have any clothes, any make-up, or my car or my cell phone charger. I don't have any cash."

"You're not going back to your house, Anita. Not now. It's going to be okay. We'll make a plan."

Protesting, she said, "But, I need some clothes. These sweats, as stylish as they may be, will suffice for now but I need … oh, I feel so lost." She paused and took a sip of tea, then a deep breath. Her hands caressed the tea cup. Tears tracked down her cheeks.

Barbara softly spoke. "Anita, there's some quaint boutiques by the beach house. We'll go shopping, get some clothes there. No one will know you there."

"You're so practical but, the last thing I want to do is complicate your life with my problems."

"Nonsense. It will be good for you to get away, to think and to have some girl time. Thomas and I love you. You're part of our family, in fact, the daughter we never could have. Helping is part of loving."

"But," she stammered, "I need to go to the bank. I need some undergarments. What about my car? I don't even have my car." Her gaze settled down on the tiled floor. "Maybe I should call Officer Morrison and have him meet me at the house on Monday when Daryl is at work."

Thomas retorted. "No. That's not a good idea. Daryl might come home early. You don't know what frame of mind he's in or what he might do. John told me to have you get an emergency restraining order in place before you face Daryl. It gives the police permission to keep Daryl at a safe distance."

"Let me think. Let me think." Anita put her tea down, brought both hands to the sides of her face, and lowered her head.

Barbara reached up lightly touching Anita's hand and cheek. "I don't think it's a good idea to go to the house now. How about we ask Susan to pick up some things for you? We could ask Officer Morrison to accompany her." She turned toward Thomas for reassurance.

Thomas interjected a bit gruffly, "I still think a restraining order is best."

Their conversation was interrupted by the ringing of the telephone on the other side of the kitchen. Thomas rose and answered it.

"Hello, Doctor Kirkland."

Anita and Barbara were silent. They could faintly hear a man's voice on the line.

"Daryl?" Thomas, with wide opened eyes, his brow creased, quickly turned to face Anita and Barbara. He brought his finger to his lips to signal, *be quiet*, shaking his head, drawing their attention. "Daryl?" he repeated more loudly.

Barbara and Anita turned to Thomas, eyes intently watching, listening carefully to the one way conversation.

Thomas said, "Yes, she called me late Friday night. She said she had a family emergency and had to leave town for a few weeks. She asked if I could handle the practice while she's gone. What's going on?"

Anita and Barbara could not make out Daryl's words. Thomas signaled with his hand a circular gesture signaling come on. Get the made up story out.

Anita and Barbara heard only Daryl's muffled voice. Thomas shuffled his weight from one foot to the other, rolling his eyes. "No, I haven't heard from her since Friday night but she told me she wouldn't be able to fill me in for a few days."

Thomas pointed his finger at his temple, circling it around indicating, crazy. Anita draped her fingers through her hair; perspiration formed on her forehead.

"She didn't go into any details."

Anita and Barbara stared at Thomas, straining to hear Daryl, their bodies stiff with anxiety, tension and fear. "I have to go now. I just got called to the hospital. Bye."

When Thomas hung up the phone, Anita was shaking. Her jaw locked and teeth clenched. "Oh my god. He called here. He's looking for me here. What did he say? I don't want to get you more involved. I don't know what he might do."

Thomas walked toward the kitchen table. His brow was furrowed and his eyes locked with Anita's. "He wanted to know if I heard from you, and when I told him you were going to be out of town for a few weeks, he seemed to believe me. I don't think he suspects you're here or that we know anything. I'm not taking any chances."

Thomas neatly folded the morning's paper. "We're packing up a few things for you and Barbara right now and you're heading to the beach house. We can worry about your clothes later. Right now, I want you to call John Osborn for an emergency restraining order. You should take care of that first." His eyes narrowed in concern. "We can call Officer Morrison later and have him accompany Susan to your house to pick up some things when Daryl isn't there, but it's going to wait until I'm sure you're safe. Why don't you and Barbara make a list of what you need while I get John on the phone?"

"Thomas, I don't know …"

"Really, Anita. I'm not comfortable with what is happening and I don't want to put Barbara at risk. I want you to go to the beach house with her. He doesn't know where it is. You will be safe there."

Barbara stood. "I'll get some paper and a pen so we can make a list of what Susan should bring. I'll help you, Anita. If you get the restraining order, the police will be able to keep him away from you. Look in the mirror. Look what he did to you. Next time you might not be able to walk way. You've got to do this. We're not going to let Daryl hurt you again. Let's call John."

"Now?"

Barbara tenderly wrapped her arms around Anita. "Yes, it's time. Now."

TWELVE

ANITA SHAKILY GOT UP FROM THE TABLE AND looked into Barbara's caring eyes. "May I talk to you?"

"Of course. What is it?"

"Let's go into the bedroom. I feel a little light-headed." Barbara held Anita around the waist as she slowly stood up. Thomas went over to the counter looking for Attorney John Osborn's phone number. "I'm going to get John on the line," he said.

Barbara stopped and turned toward her husband. "Thomas, please wait just a moment. Let me talk with Anita. She's upset. Please give us some time."

"Okay, but I'm doing everything I can to make sure the two of you are safe. John will help us through this process." He fumbled through the address book.

"I know, honey. Just give us a minute. I'll be right back." Together the women tottered into the spare bedroom where Anita collapsed onto the bed and started crying. "I'm so afraid."

Barbara sat next to Anita and hugged her tightly. "I understand, at least I think I do. Are you more injured than you're letting on? The emotional toll must be overwhelming."

Staring, with tears dripping down her cheeks, she looked at Barbara. "I'm not sure you can fully understand what is going on here." Anita's whole body was shaking. She lay down and curled up into a ball. "I haven't told anyone the whole story, what's really been going on. I was too afraid people would judge me; too embarrassed." She gulped for air. "I got this black eye and fractured eye socket because I wanted to take a bath. Take a bath. How can you possibly understand? If I file a restraining order what will it do? Keep me safe? You've got to be kidding. The restraining order is just a temporary thing. He …" Uncontrollably sobbing in Barbara's arms, Anita was barely able to talk. "I'm so afraid but I know for sure that a restraining order will infuriate Daryl, like a red cape before a bull, egging him on, challenging him—gasoline on a fire. Please listen, please …"

Anita reached for a tissue on the nightstand and wiped her dripping nose. Haltingly, she inhaled, her sobs subsiding. "I married Daryl. I thought I loved him. He was good for me for a while. He … Barbara, how can you get it? Thomas is everything on the outside that he is on the inside. Daryl is not like that. I thought he was but I know he's not. He's got an evil side."

"Anita, what are you suggesting? You're scaring me."

"I know I want to leave him. I know we're not good for each other. I know all that but I'm scared to death that he could … he could kill me. Look at what happened to Nicole Brown Simpson. But, I'm thinking if I can convince him that I'm not good for him, that we're doing the right thing by being apart, maybe, just maybe, I can get on with my life and he with his without all this drama and fear. I've seen how he reacts right after these violent episodes. Usually he's remorseful for short periods so I want to strike … try to convince him … while the iron is hot, while he's still remorseful."

Barbara said, "What are you suggesting?"

"I want to call him and see if I can convince him to leave on his own, without restraining orders, without police intervention."

Barbara sat up stiffly. "Anita, are you serious?"

"Yes, very much so. I can't expect you to understand the dynamics of this relationship. He once beat me up because I smiled at the grocery clerk— smiled at a grocery clerk. And another time saying I flirted with a guy in the elevator. He's so jealous and possessive. He's beaten me because I made rice instead of potatoes for dinner—and you expect him to leave me alone once he hears I'm filing a restraining order against him?" She said, "It's not that easy, Barbara. It's not logical. He's not logical."

Barbara shook her head. "What could you possibly say to him? I don't like this at all."

"First, I'll try to convince him to leave because it's better for him—not casting blame. Barbara, I need to do this. I need to try this first before I get attorneys involved. Let me try."

"It doesn't sound like a good idea to me. You're right about me not understanding the mentality of someone who would do this to you. But, listen to me." Barbara softly put her hands on Anita's shoulders and looked straight at her swollen face. "You can't call him now. He just spoke to Thomas and that would tip him off that Thomas knows where you are. He could blame us—say we're trying to talk you out of going back to him. I'm afraid too. We've got to be careful."

"Okay, okay. That makes sense but I still think I may be able to get out of this without a restraining order."

Clumsily Anita sat upright and ran her fingers through her hair, trying to make sense of dread. Her breathing was short, uneven. Her mouth was cotton-ball dry, making it difficult to swallow. "Wait Barbara, there's more. Andy told me to be watching out for double vision. I have it. There are two of you right now. I need to see Andy. I need to find out why I have double vision."

"Oh my god, Anita. And you want to talk to this

monster that beat you? Really? Really?" Barbara rubbed her head, "We need to call Andy and see if he wants you to go to the ER or if he thinks you can wait until Monday to see him in his office. Regardless, we need to get away from this house because I'm not convinced Daryl won't come here. He called the house looking for you. What will he do next? Call Andy right now and then pack a few things. I'm not bringing you back here. I'm either taking you to the emergency room or to the Best Western just outside of town. Then, the two of us are heading to the Pajaro Dunes beach house."

Anita nodded in agreement. "I'll call Andy now. And, I'd like to call Susan and Officer Morrison too. I liked your idea of Susan going to pick up my things. We'll ask Officer Morrison if he can meet Susan at my house. I'll make a list." She hesitated, "I want to call Daryl later today. I want to. I know you don't understand but it's something I must try. "

Barbara rolled her eyes. "I don't understand and I don't like it either, but I'm beginning to understand this is bigger than I realized. Maybe you should call a counselor that could help you. I think I can get a name for you, someone who deals with domestic violence. Yes, before you call Daryl I insist that you speak to someone who knows more about this, who can help you through the process, a counselor and John."

"I'm willing to do that."

"I'll go talk to Thomas. We can make phone calls

and decisions after you see Andy and get your vision checked. I'll need to tell Thomas about your double vision and our plan to go to a hotel. He's really going to insist you file the restraining order now."

"I know … but he doesn't understand either. I think there may be a way to get Daryl out of the house and on his way without getting the police more involved."

"Anita, this is a lot for me to process. We've agreed that you're going to talk to John about the order, right? Before you call Daryl?"

Anita reached for Barbara's hand. Her crumpled and bruised body ached. "Yes, fair enough. I'll talk to him but I'm not making any decisions about it until I've had a little more time to think. My head hurts so much. I'm so scared. Thank you Barbara. Thank you for helping me."

Barbara took Anita's damp hand and squeezed it gently. She stood. "Get your things ready. Your clothes are washed and on the dresser. I've got to pack too. Let's get you to Andy and when you're safely in the hotel we can talk more about a plan."

THIRTEEN

INDEED, DR. ANDY CHEN WANTED TO SEE ANITA in the emergency room. The double vision could mean the entrapped muscle would require surgery. He didn't want her to wait until Monday.

Anita closed her swollen eyes on the car ride to the hospital. The double vision and the car ride made her nauseous. Perspiration formed on her brow. Her right arm throbbed in the cast—pulsing with each adrenal rushed heartbeat.

"I'm struggling, Barbara, struggling to hold myself together. My mind races." Anita cried, tears melting off her cheeks, dripping, unobstructed onto her pants. She desperately wanted to hold it together.

Think about what needs to be done. Think Anita, breathe and think. Calm yourself. It was hard to concentrate; sludge surrounded her brain. *With my eyesight affected, Daryl's latest punch could destroy my career. What a mess I've made of my life.*

She steadied her breathing and focused on the tasks at hand. "Tomorrow, I'd like to call Susan and Officer Morrison. I'll ask if Officer Morrison can meet her at the house. I'll make that list later."

She stuttered, her head downcast, afraid to look at Barbara. "I want to call Daryl later today. I want to. You've got to understand."

Barbara hands tensed on the steering wheel. Her neck stiffened. Her eyes focused on the familiar road. "I don't understand, no I don't. And, I don't like it either but this is much bigger than I realized. You agreed to a counselor before you call Daryl. I think I can get a name for you, someone who deals with domestic violence, and before you even think of calling Daryl let's see what Andy says about your eye. First things first."

"Yes, I'll talk to Andy. And, I know Thomas wants me to talk to John Osborn. He's been very persistent."

Barbara sighed. "He is looking out for your best interest. He's trying to protect you."

Anita's tears slowed. Her face softened. "I know how much Thomas cares about me, but he doesn't understand either. I still think there may be a way to get Daryl out of the house and on his way to a new life without getting the police involved."

"Anita, we've agreed that you're going to talk to John about the restraining order, right? Before you call Daryl?"

"I ... I'll talk to him, but I'm not making any

decisions about a restraining order until I've had a little more time to think and see what Andy says about my eye. Darn it. Darn it. My head hurts so much. My arm is in a cast. My vision's blurred. I can't think straight. My heart aches. I'm so scared." Anita's words clattered noisily on the car mats. Barbara's breath deepened as she tried to unclench her hands from the steering wheel, taking in the pain from her dear friend.

"Let's get you to the ER, Anita. Thomas and I will help you through this. We're here for you."

A new swell of tears rushed from Anita's eyes. "I want to escape and survive this intact. I want all of us to be safe." Her drained body melted. Soupy bubbles of fear washed through her.

BARBARA LED HER INTO THE EMERGENCY ROOM where they met Dr. Andy Chen. He examined Anita's eye. "It's too swollen now even if we needed to operate. Finish your antibiotics as directed and continue icing it. I want to see you back in my office in one week. The swelling should be down enough then. We'll decide then if we need to schedule surgery." His brows pulled together slightly. He gently touched the side of her arm. "Rest, Anita. Refrain from straining your eye. I advise minimal amounts of television—no more than 30 minutes at a time. No reading for at least three days." She listened intently and nodded agreement. She said nothing, her tongue gluey thick with shame.

FOURTEEN

Leaving the hospital, Barbara drove Anita to the Best Western Hotel on the other side of town.

Once they were checked in and in their room, Anita sat stiffly on the bright flowery bedspread on the edge of the double bed. Unconsciously, she rubbed her thumb and pointer finger together, an old habit from childhood she used when she was stressed. Barbara bustled around the hotel room unpacking for both of them. Anita plopped all the way down on the bed, lying sideways with her feet dangling near the floor. Barbara sat down next to her.

"I'm going to call Thomas and tell him we're here and tell him what Andy said about your eye. He'll be waiting for my call." Anita didn't move, didn't speak. She blinked back tears.

Barbara picked up the hotel phone and dialed. "Thomas, we've checked into the Best Western. We're in room 112."

"Anita most likely needs surgery on her eye but he wants to wait a week until the swelling goes down. She's to take her antibiotics, Percocet for the pain, ice packs on her eye, and rest. He bandaged her eye with an alien-looking contraption so she doesn't strain it. She has to wear it for 24 hours and then see how her vision is when she takes it off. All things considered, she's doing okay."

Anita's eyes closed. Her thoughts were muddled. She noted the tenderness in Barbara's voice as she spoke to Thomas, such a quiet ease of communication. Anita's head throbbed with pain. Her heart drummed in her chest, out of tune. She fidgeted with her fingers.

Quietly, Barbara spoke into the receiver. "Yes, I've got John's number. She agreed to talk to him." She glanced at Anita lying on the bed. "She's resting right now. I'll talk with her soon about calling him. She's out of danger. We're safe. Daryl wouldn't know to look for her here. It's been a long couple of days. By the way, there is left over pot roast in the refrigerator for dinner. We're fine. Really, we're fine. I love you. Talk to you later tonight."

Softly, Barbara hung up the phone. She went over to the bed where Anita was laying awkwardly with her legs still dangling near the floor. She placed her legs on the bed. "Are you cold? Let's get you all the way in bed so you can rest. That position doesn't look too comfy. I'll close the drapes so you can sleep. Do you need a Percocet? I'll get you one and a glass of water."

Barbara gave Anita a Percocet. "Do you want some ice for your eye or would you rather rest a bit?"

Anita replied, "I'll rest now. We can do ice later."

In the darkened hotel room with their beds barely three feet apart, Barbara lay down atop the bedspread. She pulled out her reading light and a book from her small suitcase. She could almost feel Anita's air pushing up from her lungs desperately trying to calm her. She tried to focus on *Gift from the Sea* by Anne Morrow Lindbergh, but Anita's restlessness had her on alert. She read the same paragraph over and over. The words on the pages were slippery; their meanings not catching and holding in her brain. Anita finally dozed. Barbara sensed every twitch in her friend's body; every twist and turn that rumpled the covers and matted the pillow.

For Anita, images of Daryl jolted through her like electricity; zapped her mind, flashing lightning bolts, heating then jarring her, burning her. There were images of Daryl at the Sales conference in his perfectly pressed khaki pants.

Salesman of the Year.

Slap.

"Why were you flirting with the man in the elevator?"

Push.

Their wedding day underneath the palm trees. Tender kisses and love-making on their honeymoon in Lake Tahoe.

"Why did you flirt with the waiter?"

Smack.

At a picnic in the redwoods sipping wine, making love in the moss underneath a grove of trees. Feeding each other strawberries.

"I wanted rice. Why did you make potatoes?"

Black eye.

Hiding the bruises.

Made-up excuses.

Apologies.

Make-up sex.

Anita drifted in and out of drugged sleep. She dreamt that she was a tiny bug tucked in a dark hole in the wet earth. She wanted to listen only to the muted sounds of earthworms digging in the rich soil, no other noise. She wanted it dark and quiet.

Barbara watched and listened as Anita's shallow breaths and restlessness gave way to even, deep puffs; rhythm of the waves, ebbing and flowing. The covers finally remained settled. Sleep at last.

Two hours passed before Anita stirred. Barbara looked up from her book. "You awake, Sunshine?"

"Yes." Anita answered and with a throaty voice still trying to purge the heavy fog of sleep. "You always call me Sunshine even when I don't feel so bright."

"You are sunshine to me, young lady, even in the

most difficult of times. Don't you ever forget it."

Anita woozily sat up. Nausea overwhelmed her. She had a dull, heavy ache in her arm. Barbara walked over to the heavy drapes. "I'll let the other sunshine in our room." She pulled on the plastic rod. The sunlight temporarily blinded them. The trees swayed. Their spent russet, curled leaves swirling around the ground.

"It's still day time? What time is it?" Anita asked.

"Time to make some decisions. I promised Thomas I'd give you John's phone number when you woke up. He's been in Family Law a very long time and is one of Thomas's best friends; a golfing buddy too. He's seen everything in his thirty plus years in family law. He'll give you some sound advice. He'll walk you through this process. Thomas assured me John wouldn't mind if you called him on Sunday. In fact, he's expecting your call. Please call him. I can leave the room if you prefer privacy."

"No, it's okay. The cat is out of the bag. The dam is broken and you might as well sit here and hear the whole story. Let me dust off some cobwebs in my brain first. How about a diet Coke from the vending machine first? I need something with caffeine."

"Of course. One cobweb-clearing diet Coke coming right up, Dr. Stone." Barbara left the room.

She returned with Anita's drink.

After sipping it, Anita's trembling hands reached for the phone. She dialed the number on the scratch pad Barbara handed to her.

When John Osborn answered, Anita stuttered, "John, John Osborn. It's Doctor Anita Stone. I got your phone number from Dr. Thomas Kirkland."

"Hi, Dr. Stone. I've been waiting for your call. How are you doing? Are you somewhere safe?"

"Yes. I don't think Daryl would know to look for me here."

"Dr. Stone, in light of what Thomas has told me, there is definite cause for a Temporary Restraining Order or TRO as we call it."

Haltingly, Anita replied, "I know you and Thomas think a restraining order is best, but do you really think a piece of paper is going to stop him? You're not in my situation. He used to beat me because I didn't water the plants on Thursday. He's not rational. So, how exactly can a restraining order possibly stop him if he wants to get to me? I'm afraid of him, but I don't want to pour fuel onto the fire."

"There are steps we can take. Believe me, Dr. Stone, I have seen everything. The courts have seen countless cases of domestic abuse. There is a process we need to follow. I'd really like to speak with you in person to explain further. There is a lot we can do to protect you."

"I'm not sure that piece of paper is any good, but, well, I promised Thomas that I would talk to you but—"

John interrupted. "I can meet you at the hotel so I can explain your rights. It's to protect you and, from what I understand, this might be what is best at this point. A TRO buys you time, puts a distance between you and your abuser. I'd like to get more details. I've known Thomas over thirty years and he's worried for your safety. He's not one to panic. May I come meet you?"

Anita sighed, "Yes, but, I'm not feeling that well." She hesitated. "Things are happening too fast. I've had some pain meds. My head and arm still hurt and my vision is blurred."

"From your injury?"

"Yes."

"That's precisely why we should do this quickly."

Her thoughts serpentined through her head, curvy and tangled, but she finally agreed. "Okay. You can come over so we can talk."

"I know where it is. I can be there in half an hour."

Anita turned toward Barbara, "Can you meet John Osborn in the lobby in thirty minutes? I don't want to go down to the lobby."

"Of course."

Speaking back into the phone Anita said, "Yes, John. Barbara Kirkland will meet you in the lobby in half an hour."

Anita hung up. With eyes downcast, Anita gently shook her head, the tape on her bandaged eye pulling the hairs at her temple. She spoke softly. "I still can't believe it has gotten to this. Things seem so surreal. I'm so embarrassed. I wish this was all over." Regret shrouded her. She fell back on the bed.

Barbara picked up her book from the night stand and headed for the door. "I'll give you some space and go down and wait for John. You can freshen up."

"Thanks."

When the door closed behind Barbara, Anita tossed on the bed, thrashing. The cast on her right arm was cumbersome and felt lead weighted. Conflicting emotions bombarded her brain. *What should I do now? How do I do this? How can I manage Daryl and keep him from getting angrier and more dangerous? I need to get back to work.*

Anita gently rolled over in the bed, groggy, and sat up on the edge. Her eye throbbed with every beat of her heart. She picked up the phone, dialed her home number and waited for Daryl to answer.

FIFTEEN

TINY BEADS OF SWEAT FORMED ON THE EDGE OF her hairline. There was a huge dinosaur war in her stomach; thrashing tails and tumbling bodies. After three rings Daryl picked up the phone.

"Hello."

Her voice came out raspy, "Daryl?"

"Oh, baby. Where are you? I've been so worried about you. When are you coming home? You need to come home."

Anita imagined Daryl standing in the kitchen. His chest puffed. *Now he's begging me to come home.* "Daryl, listen to me." Although she was determined to get the words out, it sounded as though they were squeezed through a mouthful of cotton balls. "I'm really injured. This has gotten out of hand. We're not right for each other."

"What do you mean? Of course we are.

Remember all the fun times we've had together?" His voice was tight like when he had a smirk on his face. "Come on, baby. I want you back home where you belong.

"It wasn't always fun, Daryl." Anita shifted uncomfortably on the bed, the pounding in her temple jack-hammering her thoughts.

In his velvety pitch, Daryl said, "Oh, come on now. Sure, we're still adjusting to each other. I didn't mean to hurt you. I'm sorry. I'm so sorry. And, I've been so worried about you. Come home. We'll work this out. We can do it. It was just bad timing. I know I had too many cocktails Friday night, but that won't happen again, I promise." She heard his stomping footsteps on the Spanish tile in their kitchen echoing in the phone.

"No, this isn't the only time this has happened. We need to part ways." Her voice was now steadier; cotton balls dissolved.

"What are you talking about? That's crazy talk."

Anita sat up straight. Her voice clear. Air pushed up through lungs giving her the strength to continue on. "No, it's not crazy. Think about it Daryl. Think about all the times this has happened. I'm not doing this anymore."

"Doing what?"

"Putting myself in a situation where you can hurt me—letting you lay a hand on me. I have some serious injuries this time." She enunciated clearly, "It's *not* happening again."

"Baby, the other night was just bad timing. I was tired and I had too much to drink. You have been so pre-occupied with work. We haven't spent much time together and I was missing you. Come on, Baby, I'll come get you. We'll work this out. Let's take a vacation so you can relax. We've been talking about going back to Paris. Let's plan that."

"Daryl ..."

He continued on, not listening to her. "Let me hold you; show you how much I love you. We'll have some drinks and a nice dinner. It'll be okay."

She took a deep breath. *He can't get to me. I'm done with this. I want this over.* "Daryl, stop. This is serious." A hint of shakiness developed in the back of her throat. She swallowed deeply.

"Where are you? Tell me where you are?"

"Daryl, listen to me. We're just not right for each other. Let's go our separate ways and remember the good times."

"Baby, are you okay? This is crazy talk, Anita. Go our separate ways? We can have many more happy times together. I love you. I need you." There was a long pause. Anita imagined Daryl's upper lip turned into a snarl. "You're not getting others involved in our lives are you? You should listen to me. I'm your husband, damn it." Anita heard a thump, possibly Daryl kicking the wall. His voice grew husky and loud. "Listen to me. We're just going through an adjustment period. It will get better. I promise. Now, stop this crazy talk and come home."

"No. Daryl, it's time for you to listen to me. We can do this the easy way or the hard way—with attorneys involved—but I'm not coming home. You need someone else in your life that can devote more time to you. I'm so busy with my practice, I'm not what you need." Anita sighed and heard the wind rustle up the leaves outside her window. "I want you to pack your things tonight and leave the house. We're not right for each other, Daryl. We're like water and oil."

"What are you saying? Of course we're right for each other ..."

Anita interrupted. "Daryl, you've got to leave. No more. Pack your things and leave. Come on Daryl. I'm serious. This isn't easy for me either but it's time. You know it and I know it. No more. No more hurt." Although the words were coming out of her mouth in a steady stream, her chest was gripped in a vise, her hair tense and her jaw clenched.

Sounding like a sorry lost little boy, he said, "I'm not leaving. This is my house. You're not kicking me out of my home.

"I bought the house with my mom's life insurance and ..."

"Anita, you're acting crazy." His voice was mean and snarly.

"No, I'm not." Her chest heaved upward gathering fresh air and resolve and she spilled out the words. "I'm not crazy and you're not going to intimidate me anymore. I have some very serious injuries. I can't even practice medicine right now. You've gone way over the line. The easy way or the hard way, Daryl? You pick. I won't be put in a box like Nicole Simpson."

"You're crazy."

"No, I'm not."

She banged the handset down and plopped back on the bed. Her heart gushed with adrenalin-rich blood. She shuttered, took a deep breath, closed her eyes, and slowly exhaled.

SIXTEEN

THOMAS WAS RESTING IN HIS EASY CHAIR, BLINKING at the television and finishing his cup of chamomile tea when he heard a knock on the door. He wasn't expecting anyone. He had just hung up with Barbara who had told him that Anita and John had met and that Anita had finally reluctantly agreed to file an Emergency Restraining Order.

Thomas walked over to the kitchen wall and pushed the lever on the intercom in the kitchen. "Hello?"

"Thomas, its Daryl." Thomas furrowed his brow. His hands shook when he heard Daryl's voice. His back stiffened. He took a deep breath, collecting himself. *Why is he here? Yesterday I told him I didn't know where Anita was? Had he suspected I was lying? Thank God Anita and Barbara are gone, safe at the hotel.* "Daryl, what is it?"

"May I come in?" He asked, his husky voice firm and flat as a board.

"What's going on?" Thomas refused to walk down the hall toward the front door.

"Anita and I had an argument and it got out of hand. I'm worried about her."

Thomas's chest tightened. "Why are you here and why are you telling me all this?"

"Thomas, I want to talk."

"No. I'm busy finishing up with some patient charts," he lied. "We don't have anything to discuss."

"Anita didn't seem herself when she left. You haven't heard from her?"

"No. I told you yesterday that she said she wouldn't call for a few days, later in the week, so I don't expect to hear from her until then." He took a deep breath. He glanced at his evening tea cooling on the end table. "That's what I know. Daryl, I can't help you. You should leave." Thomas heard the rapid thumping in his chest as he lied once again. "Daryl, I've got to go."

Daryl pleaded, "You'll ask her to call me if she contacts you?"

"I don't expect to hear from her. I've got to go. Good-bye." He switched off the intercom and unsteadily walked back to the family room. *Daryl is looking for her. I need to call Barbara and advise her to tell the front desk that no one is to give out their room number.*

Thomas sat down in his leather chair; his heart tapping like a bunch of busy elves hammering on wooden toys during the Christmas rush. He sat thinking. *Should I call the police? What will I tell them?*

A heavy weight pressed down on his shoulders. He rubbed his forehead, took off his glasses, set them on the table, and let his mind calm. After several minutes he padded down the white oak floor of the hallway and peered through the front door peephole to see if Daryl was still there.

There was no sign of him.

SEVENTEEN

S USAN HAD BEEN THE OFFICE MANAGER FOR DR. Thomas Kirkland for twenty years. After Anita joined the practice they formed a close bond. She not only ran the office and expertly managed the staff with a firm no-nonsense yet caring approach, but she helped orchestrate Anita's personal life when things got busy. She bought Anita comfortable shoes when her feet ached after long surgeries and purchased elegant gifts for Anita's friends when Anita ran behind schedule and couldn't get out of the office. Although Susan was now a close friend, she did not know the extent of discord in the Stone household. She had suspected that Daryl had been abusive in the past.

Anita had asked her to meet Officer Morrison and retrieve some clothes and things from her house.

When Susan arrived at the Stone residence,

Officer Morrison was already there. He said he had spoken with Anita and had permission to enter the house. Susan told the officer she was sure Daryl was not home as she had called his office fifteen minutes earlier and he had answered. She hung up when he answered and, since the office was more than half an hour away, he couldn't get here.

The officer banged on the front door anyway. There was no answer. He called through the door. "This is the police." There was still no answer. "We have a key. We're coming in."

Officer Morrison took the key from Susan and opened the front door. Again, he yelled, "This is the police, anyone here?"

Silence.

Officer Morrison instructed Susan to wait outside while he checked the house and to be on the lookout for any sign of Daryl. He entered the house looking around downstairs. No one was there. Cautiously he walked upstairs. The bedroom was in shambles, clothes strew about the unmade bed, the bed covers crumpled in a pile in the middle of it. Main dresser drawers were opened, some empty. One nightstand drawer was opened and emptied. The other nightstand drawer was closed. There was an empty glass and empty scotch bottle on the nightstand. He checked the walk-in closet for Daryl. He wasn't there either. The safe on the closet floor was wide open; jewelry and papers scattered on the floor.

He returned downstairs to Susan and told her no one was home. "Go ahead and get her things. The upstairs looks like it's been ransacked. It's a mess."

He waited by the front door on alert.

As instructed, Susan carefully walked into the hallway and opened the door leading into the garage. Anita's blue BMW was there. She closed the door and locked it as Anita had asked her to do. Although Daryl could still get into the garage with his garage door opener, he could not get into the house because Anita had his house key.

From the entryway Susan quickly scanned the living room and dining room. She had been in the house several times. It had always been pristine. They had a housekeeper, Hanna, who made sure things were clean and in order. This time, however, there were dirty dishes on the dining room table along with an empty wine bottle. *I wonder what happened in here and why Hanna hasn't been here to clean up. Oh my gosh, I wonder if Anita has called Hanna. She has a key. Maybe Anita should warn Hanna about coming into the house. I've got to call Anita about Hanna.*

She scurried up the stairs and into the master bedroom. She noted a fist-sized hole in the opened bedroom door. *This is new and it's not a good sign.* Susan's stomach churned at the sight of the hole. The hairs on the back of her neck prickled at attention. *What the heck happened here? My god, I hope Anita is okay. What a jerk. What an egotistical jerk.*

She had also been in the master bedroom a

couple of times previously to retrieve outfits and shoes for Anita. The room was always neat and orderly. This time, it looked like the place had been burglarized.

She hurried into the walk-in closet. There were just a few men's clothes hanging up. *Daryl must have left, packed and left in a hurry.* Rushing and frenzied, she spotted the two Samsonite suitcases tucked in the back of the closet behind Anita's dresses. She laid them flat on the floor and opened them up. She started pulling down Anita's clothes and putting them in the suitcases. She noticed that Anita's pants were separated in an awkward fashion. She noticed the empty safe. *This is very strange. Why did someone leave the safe open? And, the jewelry Anita asked me to get out of the safe is haphazardly scattered on the floor of the closet along with all these papers, probably from the safe. I do not like this.* Her heart drummed in her chest, like a jackhammer; pounding, pounding, and ricocheting off her ribs. *What would have caused Daryl to raid the safe but leave Anita's jewelry and important papers on the floor? What, exactly, was in that safe? I need to get out of here. I don't like this at all. Wait, I have to get Anita's make-up bag from the drawer by the sink and her panties and bras from her dresser drawer. Then I'm outta here.*

With trembling hands, she got Anita's make-up bag out of the bathroom and placed it in one suitcase, closed it and pulled it into the bedroom. Next to the bed she knelt down and opened the closed nightstand drawer and pulled out Anita's undergarments. As she was leaning over she noticed Anita's key ring barely sticking out from behind the nightstand. She recognized it by the medical symbol on the key ring. It was a cherished gift from Anita's mother. She picked up the keys and put them in her purse to give to Anita. She grabbed Anita's panties and bras and rushed back to the closet. She threw them on top of her other things and slammed the suitcase shut. She picked it up, charged into the bedroom, snatched the other suitcase, and hustled down the stairs.

A cannonball sized lump stuck in her throat. *I wouldn't make a good thief.* She turned to Officer Morrison still standing guard in the front of the house. Her voice was squeaky; her mannerisms jerky. "I got what she asked. The house is a disaster. It looks like Daryl is gone. His clothes aren't there. I'd like to leave now. This is creepy. Let's go."

"Sure, no problem. If Dr. Stone needs anything else, please have her call the station. Tell her that we're here to help and protect her." He locked the front door, gave Susan back the keys, took the two suitcases from her and walked to her car.

After loading the suitcases in her trunk he asked, "Are you okay, Miss?"

"Yes, I'm okay but I want to get going." Her words came out haltingly. "By the way, I know that Anita's housekeeper has a key to the house. Maybe she shouldn't be coming here by herself either."

"Have her give me a call and we'll have someone escort her to the house too."

"Okay, thanks. Thanks for your help. "Have you handled things like this before?" She said as she got into her car and rolled down the window.

"Yes. More than I care to admit. Be safe. We're here for you." He turned and walked to his squad car.

Susan drove to the parking lot at Safeway to meet up with Barbara and Anita and give Anita her belongings. Her shoulders glued to her ears, her fingers clasped the steering wheel as if choking a venomous snake.

EIGHTEEN

Susan was still anxious and nervous when she met Anita and Barbara in the parking lot at Safeway. *This must be what thieves feel like after a heist.* When she saw Anita sitting in the passenger side of the car, with dark glasses on, a bandaged eye and wearing a big garden hat, she knew Daryl must have really hurt her.

Anita rolled down the window half way. Her dark sunglasses masked most of the bruises but Susan could see her bandaged eye. She peered through the partially opened window. She noticed the cast on her right arm. "Oh my god, Anita. What happened? Are you okay? What happened to your arm?"

Anita rolled down the window all the way. "Susan, I can't really talk right now," she said quietly. Anita pulled her hat down further on her face. Dismissively, Anita waved her left arm. "I'll be fine. I have some good doctors taking care of me."

"What's going on?" Susan asked. "Your house is a disaster."

Barbara was out of the car ready to retrieve Anita's belongings. "Let's just let Anita rest."

Anita curled her head down.

"What else can I do to help?" Susan voice came out purring-kitten soft.

Quietly, Anita said, "The one thing you can do is not talk to anyone about this. I need you to do that for me." Anita's pale face radiated trepidation.

"Of course, but—"

Barbara interjected, "Daryl really hurt her and she's recovering. You need to be careful yourself and not tell anyone about this. Were you able to get everything Anita asked for?"

"Yes, yes I was." Susan walked over to her car and pulled out the luggage. "Here's what she asked me to get." Barbara opened the trunk of her cream colored BMW and Susan put the suitcases in the trunk. Then she walked back to the passenger side door and turned to Anita. "By the way, I found your keys behind the nightstand. I recognized them from the medical symbol." She reached into her purse, pulled them out and handed them to Anita. "I thought you might want them."

"Oh, thank you. I misplaced them the other night. I have been using Daryl's keys." *This is really good news. I now have both sets of keys. Daryl won't be getting into the house now.*

"Susan, did you remember to lock the door going into the garage."

"Yes." There was an awkward pause. Finally, Susan spoke up, "Uh, the house was a mess, especially the bedroom. Most of Daryl's clothes are gone."

"Oh, good." Anita sighed. "Well, it's not good that the house is a mess but I'm glad Daryl is gone. Were you able to get into the safe and get my things?"

Susan stared at the bruises around Anita's face as she looked up to talk with her. "I didn't need the combination. It was open."

"Oh, really?" Goosebumps rose on Anita's arms.

"Your jewelry was strewn all over the bottom of the closet."

"There was nothing in the safe then?"

"No. It was empty."

I knew he would take the gun. That's why I asked Susan to get my jewelry from the safe. Now I'm really in trouble. Big trouble.

She looked up at Susan. "Thanks for all your help. I really have to go. Please don't say anything to anybody. I'll call you in a couple days. Be careful too. Daryl is dangerous and he's very angry right now. Thomas is handling everything at the office until I get back." She turned toward Barbara. "Can we go?"

Susan leaned in the open passenger window. "I wish I could give you a hug. I'm so sorry. I'll hold down the fort until you return."

"Don't worry about me. I'll be fine."

"I'll be happy to help out any way I can. Oh, I

think there's something you might want to do."

"What is it?" Anita asked.

"Does your housekeeper Hanna know anything about what's going on?"

"No, I didn't think about Hanna." She looked out the car window noticing a strong wind blowing crinkly, spent leaves from the trees.

"You don't think Daryl might try to get the key from her?"

Anita rubbed her neck with her left hand. Pain shot up her spine. Her words came out like Morse code. "I'll ... call ... Hanna ... have ... her ... take a couple weeks off." A strong gust of wind blew surrounding the sedan with a whirlpool of copper-colored leaves. "I'll tell her to not give her key to him under any circumstances." Anita shook her head and rolled her shoulders. "Thank you so much, Susan. I'll be in touch when I can. I really appreciate this."

Anita turned her head forward and down, waved good-bye, and rolled up the window as Barbara slowly pulled out of the parking lot. Anita tried to focus; tried not to panic but she now knew that the gun from the safe was missing. Her chest seized. Fear shrouded her like thick, gray, wet fog. Her breath was shallow. Her head bent. Her body was aching. Her mind in anguish. *What have I done? What is going to happen now?*

NINETEEN

ANITA FIDGETED IN THE FRONT SEAT, CROSSING and uncrossing her legs, adjusting her heavy casted arm, first on the arm rest then on her door, then back on the arm rest. *I'm in real trouble now. What's he doing? Damn it!*

Barbara was aware of her friend's pain and nervousness but knew nothing about Anita's fear and anxiety over the missing gun. In her cheerful voice she said, "The beach will be relaxing. You can rest and go for walks. We'll be safe there."

"I'm so tired." Anita took off her hat and rested with her head back.

"Put the seat back and take some deep breaths. You've got the things you need out of the house. It appears that there's no reason for Daryl to go back there. Looks like he's gotten the message to move on."

If only it were that easy. He didn't sound too convinced when I talked to him. He's anything but convinced.

"Close your eyes for a while. Well, close your good eye."

"Very funny." Anita picked up her hat from her lap, placed it firmly on her head and pulled it down covering her face. She leaned the car seat back and tried to disappear into the malleable leather.

Barbara turned on some soft jazz, filling the car with tranquil music and headed onto the freeway. Two hours into the ride Anita stirred and stretched. They were on a narrow curvy road. The sky was brilliant, the clouds light and dreamy.

"Hi, Sleepyhead. We're almost there," Barbara said as she heard Anita stir.

Anita's awakening attitude had changed along with the flora. Scatterings of carpeted purple ice plant and Italian Cypress led the way. This way, this way to relaxation, rest, safety, they prompted.

Barbara rolled down the windows. "Can you smell the ocean? There's something about the heavy, salty air that is refreshing. I love this smell." She took a deep breath. Anita did too.

"Nothing like the salty ocean air and rhythm of the waves to rejuvenate your soul.," Barbara said.

She turned onto the rural road and pulled up to the guard house. The warm sun shone through the windshield, blinding Anita through her dark glasses. She pulled her hat further down her bruised face.

Rosalinda, the perky gatekeeper, greeted the pair.

Her bleached blonde hair danced in the sunlight as she spoke. "Hi, Mrs. Kirkland. It's nice to see you again. How long will you be staying?" Anita was in the passenger seat with her head down, floppy hat covering most of her face and dark sunglasses on.

"Rosalinda, it's nice to see you. My friend Anita and I will be here for about a week."

"No, Dr. Thomas?"

"No, not this time."

"Enjoy you girl's get-away."

"Thank you, we will."

"Rosalinda, if anyone asks for us, we're not here."

"Of course. Our policy is not to give out any information about any guests." She closed the sliding window to the guard house.

The heavy metal gates swung open to let them in. Barbara drove through the gate and parked the car in the garage and the two of them made their way into the beach house.

TWENTY

ANITA WAS UNPACKING IN THE SPARE BEDROOM when Barbara entered. She handed her a small gift, wrapped in simple baby blue paper. There were subtle wave designs imprinted in sea blue. Anita opened the gift revealing a small writing journal with the words, "My Beach Thoughts" written across the front.

"Now, put your sandals on and head to the beach. I've got the rest covered. I insist that you go talk to the waves and listen to the pelicans. Nothing calms the soul like the serenade of the waves. Nothing relaxes the body like sand massaging the bottoms of your feet. If you feel inclined, jot down your thoughts."

"I'll take you up on that." Anita grabbed her flip flops from the closet, a pen from her purse, and headed out the sliding glass door.

The stretch of beach outside the Kirkland beach house was stamped with just a few footprints including Anita's. There were diamonds shining on the waves, foam rolling, churning the vast expanse of water. Anita sat barefoot on a towel, cross-legged, journal and pen in hand. The ocean melted into the clear sky; sapphire on sapphire. Waves pelted the shore. She was lost in thought. She wrote:

The Healing Beach
I totter to ocean
Slow motion
Letting waves tumble,
Rumble
My feet salty wet
Help me forget

Anita's thoughts turned toward her mom. Her absence still felt like Anita was missing a limb with phantom pain radiating throughout her entire body. *Mom, what would you say to me now? Please speak to me, wrap your loving arms around my body. Help this hurt go away. Help me heal. Tell me what to do.*

She heard a soft whisper. She closed her eyes. Louise's voice came to her as clearly as though she were sitting next to her. Anita was still. The air inside her lungs and surrounding her body somehow moved differently; calmer, warmer, and smoother. It was the same blissful feeling she had as a young child when her mother tucked her in bed at night.

Anita, my daughter, I have told you on many occasions that you are beautiful and strong and wise and loved. Remember the story of Dr. Elizabeth Blackwell, the first woman to earn a medical degree in America? It wasn't easy for her. She paved new roads. Don't let Daryl spoil your dreams. He's just a pothole. You can navigate around it and put this all past you. If I've given you anything that is a part of me, it is courage and strength. You can get out of this. Listen to your soul for direction. Listen to the waves. I am here, right beside you. You will make the right choice now and follow it. Go with your gut. Have the courage to do what needs to be done so that all your dreams can come true.

A feeling of tranquility and calm enveloped Anita. The moist air, perfumed with sea salt and hints of seaweed, soothed her nostrils. Her jaw relaxed as the breeze surrounded her body and lifted her spirits. She soared on the clouds of possibilities, rode the waves of decisions; letting them tumble on the shore then releasing the bad ones to absorb back into the sand.

Barbara's soft footsteps in the sand broke her serenity. "I brought us a little picnic—sandwiches for the soul. May I sit down?" Barbara asked.

"Of course, my friend. I was deep in thought." Her feet were buried in the gritty, warm sand.

Barbara set the old-fashioned, wicker picnic basket down, opened up the flaps and pulled out a beach towel. She kicked off her shoes and relaxed down on the towel close to her friend. They each stared into the ocean.

"Thomas and I love it here. I think we finally figured it out."

"Figured what out?"

"Why we love it here, sitting in the sand, listening to the waves, the beach sounds. It smooths all the rough edges. Our breath comes out deeper, easier. Our thoughts come cocooned in velvety reason instead of intertwined in judgment. We relax into them instead of against them."

The women watched a squadron of pelicans. First they flew in a V-formation toward the water. Then, a few stragglers at the ends released and soared closer to the water. Without disturbing the velocity, they again joined the squadron in precisely their designated spots and scooped up and away.

"Isn't it amazing how they do that?" Anita asked.

"I never get tired of it. That's part of the beach rhythm. It's a calming place—a place to get lost in your thoughts. Isn't it so beautiful?" Barbara stared out at the glittering water.

"Yes, with each wave I'm really trying to find myself more at ease." She turned to Barbara. "But I miss my mom so much. Maybe it is better that she is not here to see me like this. I've really messed things up this time." She bowed her head. Shame came flooding back through her.

"Your mother would understand. Anita, very few people make it from A to Z without a few side trips."

"That's an interesting way to put it, but these side trips I've been making are major detours, not Sunday scenic country drives." She shook her head, trying to settle her muffled mind. "You talk about A to Z. I don't even know where A and B are, let alone Z." Her cheeks sank, her words melted with insecurity. She morphed back into a lonely little girl again.

"You'll find your way. This is a place that will help you." She scooted closer to Anita. "Here's what I know about you. You're kind and compassionate. You're a caring woman—a healer, a gifted orthopedic surgeon." She watched as Anita's brow softened. "You have the respect of the community and your fellow physicians. Thomas and I love you like a daughter." Anita's breath slowed to the rhythm of Barbara's. "Your staff thinks the world of you. You didn't get to be an orthopedic surgeon by giving up. It was a rough haul in medical school. This is just a blip on the screen. I promise you, Anita, you will get through this and find your way."

Anita let out a huge sigh.

Barbara said, "I just read something in this book, *Gift from the Sea,* by Anne Morrow Lindbergh. I think it's very relevant to you. Let me find it." Barbara pulled out the little book and thumbed through the pages. "Here it is. The essay doesn't all pertain to your current situation, but there is one sentence that I believe is important to think about. Anne writes, 'One must lose one's life to find it.' I think that's what is happening to you, Anita. Even though you might not know it yet, you need to lose your old life to find your bearings again."

Anita sat composed as warm, wet tears trickled down her cheeks.

Barbara turned her gaze away from Anita and stared out at the glittering water. Another squadron of pelicans glided by. "I've taken a few side trips in my life. I promise you, you will get through this. My course wasn't as straight and narrow as you might think. I once drove to hell and back when I was in my twenties, followed by footsteps of floundering. You're not the first person to wander into dark jungles without a machete or a flashlight, but you'll make it. I did." Barbara smiled at her friend.

Anita grinned, wiping her cheeks with the back of her hand. "You went to hell and back? I'm shocked."

"Oh, sure. This prim and proper, retired high school principal was once on a road to—well, let's just say, it wasn't Disneyland. There were no Tinker Bells at the place I was headed."

Anita playfully kicked sand over onto Barbara's bare toes. "No Tinker Bell? How could that be? I can't imagine such a place. No Disneyland? No Tinker Bell?"

Barbara nodded her head. "Yes, there are places like that. I found a few of them in my younger days. Fortunately, I was rescued by a hypothetical tow truck driven by a wonderful man. You now know him by the name of Thomas Kirkland. That kind man put fuel in my car, fixed my tires, and helped me exit a long, potholed stretch of a dark highway." Her voice got more chipper as she announced. "He's my very own AAA." Then she giggled softly.

Anita grinned. "You're so funny. Thomas driving a rescue tow truck. Wait until I tell him that you fantasize about him being a tow truck driver. Somehow I can't see him dressed in grubby overalls with grease under his nails. Thomas the tow truck driver has a certain ring to it."

"Not literally." She raised her eyebrows.

"I know, but you must admit it does sound good."

Giggling more loudly, Barbara lifted the flap of the picnic basket, pulled out a faded red checkered tablecloth, and spread it between them. "Now, may I offer you one of these soul sandwiches? They look a lot like cream cheese and cucumber, but its magic cream cheese. It will take us where rapid healing can take place, easing the pain where solutions become obvious and where fear is replaced by action. And, maybe, just, maybe we'll find Tinker Bell soaring above us."

Anita reached out her hand. Barbara placed the magical sandwich in her palm with all the care as if it were a newborn kitten.

Mesmerized by the waves, comforted by the warmth of the sun, they savored their lunch.

After lunch, which included not only the sandwiches but a few green olives, slices of Fuji apples, and lemonade, Barbara packed up the picnic basket and stood up. "I'm going to put the basket away and take a little rest. Are you coming in?"

"I think I need a few more minutes of sunshine. I'll be up in a few minutes. I have some things I want to write down in my new journal."

"No problem. Enjoy the warmth of the sunshine." Barbara picked up the picnic basket.

"Thank you for the lovely lunch. Look," Anita pointed to the water with her left hand. "I think I see Tinker Bell coming in on a wave."

"I think I see her too. You just never know." Anita watched Barbara stroll back to the beach house leaving her alone with her thoughts. She added to her poem, "The Healing Beach," in her journal. The words floated down in whispers into her hands.

> Chilly water cools distress
> Dissolving hurt
> Into minute minutia
> Meaningless
> Harsh memories erased
> Calm finds its place

Anita rested the pen on the journal and lay back on the beach towel, but her thoughts wouldn't still, coming in waves. She had to keep writing.

> Listening, I hear shouts
> Therapeutic thunder
> It screams,
> "A new life, the old one asunder."
> My toes covered in sand
> Upright I stand.

INSIDE THE BEACH HOUSE BARBARA EMPTIED THE picnic basket and retreated to her bedroom. She laid down on the aqua satin bedspread pulling a handmade quilt over her. As she rested she thought of her time at UC Berkeley.

TWENTY-ONE

BARBARA HAD TO ASK A GUY TO HER HIGH SCHOOL senior prom. That was really humiliating, especially since she wanted John, her homework partner, to ask her. They spent two afternoons a week working on projects together at each other's houses, and Barbara thought she was in love. John apparently thought otherwise. He told her he asked Sherry to prom.

Barbara was more than offended. She remembered Sherry who singlehandedly brought down the average test score of the junior class. She had long, gorgeous legs stopping just shy of her immense boobs. She kicked high enough at football games for guys to get a peek at her "soft spot" as John used to call it.

Since John was going to the prom with Sherry,

Barbara asked the only decent other guy who wasn't going, Eric. He was nice enough but she had an awful time watching John with his hands all over Sherry. Things weren't much better in the romance department the rest of junior and senior years. Upon high school graduation, Barbara was offered scholarships to three schools. She chose Berkeley to the chagrin of her parents.

Berkeley was the perfect place for a girl to let her hair down, especially one who had been so studious all through high school. That was Barbara, "Miss four-eyes," aka "P & P" for prim and proper. She had graduated in the top two percent of her high school class and was proud of it, but she was still envious of all the attention the other girls got. You know the ones. They didn't have to work for their golden hair, big boobs and dumbness, but the boys seemed to like them.

At UC Berkeley there was a party almost every night, with lots of beer and lots of good looking guys too, both bad and good. The kids didn't know about Barbara's scholastic scholarship and she didn't tell them. Unlike most freshmen who gain weight their first year, Barbara actually lost ten pounds. It was as if she shed her overcoat. She wore padded bras and bleached her hair lighter, much to her parent's disapproval. There was a new lighter, energized Barbara. There were no curfews, lots of booze, grass, and bad boys. It was enough to purge her P&P image. She was having a blast.

Barbara managed to hold it together on her weekly Sunday calls from her parents. Usually she was nursing a hang-over, but she didn't think her parents suspected anything. She had been a model high school student; an "angel" in their eyes her freshman and sophomore years at Berkeley, but in the fall of her junior year she started dating Pete Hancock. He was a tall, lanky boy with unruly sun-bleached hair which matched his unruly outlook on life and electric smile that generated a lot of attention from the girls. He was in his sixth year at UC Berkeley having changed majors three times, now concentrating on some sort of Liberal Arts degree or something similar with a huge emphasis on "liberal."

Pete and Barbara had gone on a drive and parked overlooking the San Francisco Bay on an unseasonably warm October night. They drank beer and smoked a few joints, all of which was Barbara's new week-end normal. This night Pete brought some LSD. He had taken it before but she wasn't convinced that she needed anything but beer and pot. That night Pete kept coaxing her saying, "It's an amazing experience. I feel so blissful on it. Come on. Making love will be fun. It's really a trip, the latest. You've got to try it. Don't be so prudish. You'll love the feeling." Finally she acquiesced; both of them licking the LSD-laced paper until it was nearly dissolved and then downing it with beer.

Nothing happened right away. They got out of the car and sat on the grass staring out at the lights of the city below and the darkness of the bay while drinking beer and making out. They went for a walk. Pete was walking a few paces in front of her and suddenly he looked like he was floating above the walking path or the path was sinking, Barbara couldn't tell which. They giggled about everything. There seemed to be a screen of changing color above the bay. It turned from jet black to cherry red and the screen started singing weird songs to her. Yes, the bay and sky were singing. She sang along giggling at the made-up words about freedom and love. Then, there was a wall of color on the dirt. It was purple and chartreuse and pink. They ran and stumbled, laughing while holding hands and singing to the moon.

Her heart beat at racetrack speed. Together, they collapsed on the damp grass, fumbled while stripping off their clothes and made clumsy love while dirt and twigs stuck to their bodies. It was awkward and thrilling and electrifying. They started and stopped sex several times; no orgasm, just pumping and grinding. They giggled at their uncoordinated bodies; each moving to a different tune. Pete said her breasts were "picture perfect and perky." It took him several tries to say it and she thought he said something about a turkey. They laughed and laughed oblivious to the hard, cold dirt and awkwardness of their coupling. Barbara never had an orgasm that night but it was quite the "trip."

Barbara spent her weekends with Pete, using drugs and drinking alcohol. During Christmas vacation Pete went home to Eureka to be with his family and Barbara went home to Ferndale. Pete's parents were divorced. His father was an attorney; his mother a free spirited coffee shop owner who wore long flowing skirts and sold pot on the side.

Barbara's parents, on the other hand, were not so free spirited, but she knew she was loved. They were very strict about school and hard work. Barbara had a babysitting job every summer from the time she was fourteen. Her dad was a doctor; a kind, soft spoken, gentle man. He came into her life after her biological father died. He adopted her and her little brother Bobby. He cared for them and loved them unconditionally. Barbara's mother worked with her dad in his office.

At home, there were strict rules about dinner; together every night at six, unless Dad was out on a house call. Her parents never seemed to get tired of each other, always holding hands and laughing at each other's very corny jokes. It was annoying and cute at the same time. Bobby, her younger brother was also home for the holidays as well as Jacob, her older step-brother who had a few days off from Stanford Medical School. Jacob and Barbara got along well.

She admired him for his steadfast determination to be a doctor. While she was floundering trying to decide what she wanted to do with her life, nothing got in Jacob's way of becoming a doctor just like his father.

Barbara's parents couldn't stop doting over Jacob

during the holiday break and reminded her that she, too, was accepted to Stanford University where she could see Jacob. Instead, she had chosen UC Berkeley.

Barbara's dad told her that Berkeley was known for "challenging conventional assumptions about science and culture." Clearly, he did not approve of her choice to go to Berkeley. "Stanford. You were accepted to Stanford. There you would be able to focus on your studies. Your brother is there. He can keep an eye on you. I've been reading a lot about protests at Berkeley. The free-thinking style is not for you."

But, that's exactly why Barbara chose Berkeley. She didn't tell her dad and mom though.

On Christmas afternoon Barbara confided to Jacob about her drug and alcohol use including her LSD trip. He couldn't believe it. "You're ruining your future. This Pete guy is no good for you. You could do anything you want. You're much smarter than I am and you choose drugs and alcohol with a loser?"

"He's not a loser."

"He's not?" he said with a smirk on his face. "He's in his sixth year of undergrad studies? Seriously, Barbara, who does that?"

Barbara sat on her childhood bed next to him digesting what he was saying but with a stiff military-straight back.

"Why are you acting so hippie-dippy?" Jacob asked. "You're throwing your life away. How can you do this to Mom and Dad? How can you do this to yourself?"

Barbara squirmed on the bed; her long, bleached hair freely flowing down her back over her loose, oversized purple blouse. She pulled her headband tighter down her forehead. "I'm tired of the establishment. The man can't tell me what to do. I want to have some fun and this is fun."

Jacob got up and tromped to the door, turned around and glared at her. "Fun? You call this fun? I call this stupid. This is very stupid. I can't believe what I'm hearing from you. Get a grip." Loudly, he slammed the door.

Those words hurt, especially coming from her brother whom she dearly admired. *Why can't he understand? He's so uptight still.*

That night she was very quiet during Christmas dinner. Dad tried to make conversation asking her the same old questions. "Are your studies going well? Have you decided what you want to do when you graduate?"

Mom was more understanding, "Art, let's enjoy the family while we are all here for dinner. Isn't it nice to have everyone home? It doesn't happen that often anymore." She turned to Barbara, handing over a dish of scalloped potatoes. "Have more, sweetheart. I know you don't get Mom's famous scalloped potatoes at college."

Bobby started balancing a spoon on his nose, but Barbara wasn't impressed with his silly antics.

Pete called right after dinner. Barbara wanted to be back with him in Tilden Park overlooking the bay; no cares, no expectations, no worries. After the call she told her parents she had a headache and went to bed.

She was sure Jacob never told her parents about her wild college days. It wasn't his nature. The following night Jacob brought home a handsome, wide-shouldered blond buddy for dinner. He was a resident at Stanford who was up visiting his aunt and doing some repairs on her front porch. His clothes were spotlessly clean and neat. He wore a Stanford sweater and loafers. He was funny and smart and they talked for hours at the dinner table, Mom and Dad, Jacob, Bobby, this guy and Barbara. She was back to her pre-college self at the dinner table and it felt good. Jacob, Bobby, and Barbara reminisced about growing up and some of the mischief they had gotten into. This new guy wasn't anything like free spirited Pete. He fit right into the family. Her parents welcomed him and Barbara liked him. He was entertaining and interesting; enjoying medicine and looking forward to his future. Mr. Stanford Sweater was easy and well-spoken, comfortable. *I bet he has a composed and soothing bedside manner.*

Mr. Sweater called Barbara when she got back to Berkeley. She thought her parents or Jacob may have put him up to it, but he insisted that they had nothing to do with it. Barbara felt like she was cheating on Pete when she first started taking his calls, but he kept the topics light and said he was just, "checking in." He lifted her spirits and they talked about everything from what was going on in school to the national news, including how Berkeley and its protests made the news. All Pete ever wanted to talk about was getting high and sex.

Late that winter Barbara started thinking more seriously about her future as she struggled trying to keep her grades up and wondering why she was hanging out with Pete. She stopped smoking weed and taking drugs, and when Pete called she told him she was having severe menstrual cramps and female issues. He didn't question her much and continued partying without her. Barbara didn't miss Pete's old crowd now that she wasn't high anymore, but she still wore her push-up bras, gauze skirts, and headbands.

She started to really look forward to her weekly calls with Mr. Stanford Sweater. They laughed and talked for hours. One day he told her she was cute, smart and funny. Pete's old charm faded rather quickly after that call. Barbara studied more and talked on the phone for hours with Mr. Stanford Sweater. He visited her and asked her to go steady during her spring break.

In her senior year Barbara transferred to Stanford with a promise of a much brighter future with Jacob's friend, Mr. Sweater. They married after he finished his residency and she became Mrs. Thomas Kirkland or as she told Anita, Thomas the tow truck driver, her rescuer.

Barbara finished with reminiscing about her days at UC Berkeley and meeting Thomas, fell into a soft, feather-and-cloud sleep dreaming of Thomas, the man she married.

TWENTY-TWO

ANITA RETURNED FROM THE BEACH, HER WHOLE demeanor lighter, and her journal in hand. After she rested, she met Barbara in the kitchen where she was preparing Fettuccini Alfredo. "Did you get a rest?" asked Barbara.

"Yes, thank you."

"You can set the table if you'd like. I have dinner covered. We're having pasta, sourdough French bread, and a salad. Nothing fancy but it will fill our tummies."

Later that evening the two women sat on Barbara's bed, clad in bright flowery, matching pajamas, and eating popcorn. Barbara had bought their flamboyant attire the day after Anita came to her house with merely the clothes on her back. Maybe the pajamas would brighten Anita's spirits and come to good use one day, just like the teenage slumber parties where giddy, pimpled girls talked into the early morning hours. Tonight seemed like the perfect night. The beach house was quiet. They were alone. A moist fog hung just above the cypress trees. The air was still and smelled a little musty.

Anita's eye looked a bit more natural tonight. The marigold-orange hue of yesterday which surrounded her eye had turned a mellow golden yellow. Above the scooped neck of her new pajamas was an angry purpled mark of an upper chest bruise where Daryl must have punched her. It was encased in blood orange and angry green hues. And, for another five weeks, the cast on her arm would be a reminder of her big defiant punch. Unlike teenage slumber parties when they quenched their thirst with Coca Cola, they each drank a chilled glass of Wente's Riva Ranch Chardonnay with their popcorn.

"Popcorn and chardonnay—it's so decadent," Anita pronounced as she raised her glass to Barbara. "Cheers, my friend. Thank you for all you've done for me."

"You're welcome." Contemplation. Barbara's lips turned upward in a grin. "I'm rather disappointed you didn't mention these lovely, lively pajamas in your toast." She tugged on the side of her top to reveal more of its vivid colors. "I looked far and wide for these." Barbara's face lit up with lightheartedness.

Anita smiled and giggled. "Oh, I was just getting to that part." Then, raising her glass for the second time, she heralded, "Here's to my dear friend whose talents I'm getting to know more about each day including, I must announce, her superb taste in fashion. She has gone to great lengths to purchase the most becoming new fashion of the day or night." And then, in a broadcast-like tone. "To Barbara Kirkland, my fashion expert who has turned this white-coated, scrub-wearing doctor by day into a runway pajama model by night."

The two women clinked glasses and fell back on their pillows in hilarity, giggling until their sides ached, careful not to spill a drop of their fine wine.

They chatted about the weather outside, about Anita loving the "feel in her bones" by the beach, and how Anita wanted a place like this, "when I finally grow up." The mood was airy and fun during their first glass of wine.

After they had eaten most of the popcorn and had another glass of wine, the conversation turned more serious.

"It wasn't always like this, "Anita said. "He swept me off my feet—this handsome, well-educated salesman with all the lines and the moves, and his gorgeous looks. He drew me in and swept me up in his waves of romance. We had some really incredible times together. I know you can't understand this, but I'd like to tell you my side of the story—how I got hooked up with Daryl. Again, I am in no way suggesting I am going back to him, but I want you to see, to understand, if you can, how this came about."

Barbara placed her empty wine glass on the table saying, "I'm here to listen. The wine helps. Should I get us another glass of wine first?"

"I think not."

"Okay. Please tell me all that's on your mind."

As a high school principal, Barbara had been trained that hearing the other side of the story, another perspective, was valuable. Everyone just wants to be heard; all her students, teachers, other administrators and now her friend. To be heard; really heard. Even if Barbara didn't agree with the rationale of who was talking, at least she knew their side of the story. So, she focused her eyes on Anita.

"You know how hard it is to get through medical school, because you know how Thomas did it. It's grueling. I think it's especially hard for a woman. I felt I had to prove myself. I had to be successful."

Anita took her last sip of wine and placed the empty glass on the nightstand. "You see," she paused as she inhaled deeply, "first my dad left when I was so young. I felt if only I had been better at school or neater ... I don't know ... maybe he wouldn't have left me—left us. I blamed myself for my dad's leaving. Of course I know now that's it's not about me. As an eight-year-old, I internalized how it would have been different if I had gotten better grades. It hurt so much that Dad didn't come visit—that he left me." Anita's bruised face was sullen but she didn't cry.

"So, I spent the next several years trying to be

the perfect child thinking maybe then he would love me, but it didn't happen. Instead he had my half-sister, Monica, and doted on her, giving her all the attention I craved. He left my mom for a woman fifteen years younger. It wasn't about me. It wasn't about my mom either. He was a selfish jerk." Anita took a deep breath.

"My dad—" After a big sigh and pause, Anita continued. "While I was in medical school, my mom finally told me what really happened. My dad had been gambling away our house payments for years and having an affair with his future, much younger, waitress-turned wife. All my craving for his affection vanished that day. I had wasted so much time. I felt so sorry for my mom. I didn't know. All these years I craved love from a man I couldn't even respect."

"Oh, Anita. That must have been hard on you, discovering that the father you pined for didn't exist. I'm so sorry."

"Yes, me too. As an adult I now think my father was a narcissist. As an eight-year-old, I didn't know that. It really hurt for many years, but I was a very good student after that. Actually, I was an ace." She smiled.

"Mom loved me with all her heart. She was such a wonderful mom. Her life revolved around me and my friends. The other kids didn't get to come to my house … um … apartment much but Mom was at every event in school. Any bake sale? Mom volunteered. Room Mother? Mom was it. Sitting in the bleachers at tennis matches in high school. Mom was always there, standing next to me. It was Mom. My mom. Oh, how I miss her." The tears welled in the corner of her eyes but she wouldn't release them. "Anyway, I made it through high school with flying colors and college too. Medical school wasn't so easy. I guess it's not easy for anyone but it was a very difficult struggle for me. I felt very lonely. All I did was study and sleep."

"So when Jack, my first husband came along, I was craving attention and wanted a normal life. He was an amazing husband, so good to me, so patient, so kind. We really were happy until Mom died so suddenly." She took a cleansing breath, her eyes downcast. "It was then that my neatly packaged world fell apart. There was no normal anymore. Jack's love should have made me feel—I don't know— comforted. Instead, his love hurt. It wasn't my mother's love. I pushed Jack away. I didn't want to be loved by him. Looking back I now realize that my relationship with him was everything I had dreamt about as a child and everything it should be. At that time I felt everyone I loved had left me because I wasn't worthy of their love."

"Oh, Anita. I'm so sorry. I know that your mom's passing was such a shock." Barbara gingerly hugged Anita. She gently held her hand up as if to halt Barbara's words and moved her arm away from her shoulder.

"Let me get this out. I want to tell you." She

took a deep sigh. "So, I alienated Jack and went on auto-pilot. I devoted my time to my practice. It was my comfort zone." She raised her eyebrows. "As you well know."

She took another deep lingering breath.

"I divorced Jack. I didn't feel worthy of his love. I couldn't return it. He didn't want the divorce, saying he was in it for the long-haul, but I wasn't. I didn't want to be loved then. When I met Daryl, it was a year after my divorce. I was tired of being the nice girl, the studious girl, the one who did as was expected. I was without a mother, a father and then, a husband. Why should I do everything I was supposed to? I was like a teenager who needed to break from her parents. I needed to break from my mold as a model citizen, a respected woman, a doctor. Daryl took me out of that comfort zone. It was such an adrenaline rush. I felt alive and naughty, something I hadn't experienced. He was such a charmer, such a bad boy."

Barbara's face stiffened.

"Let me continue. At first, he called in the middle of the afternoons telling me how much he loved me. He sent me flowers, beautiful long-stemmed ruby roses, for no reason. He was spontaneous and vibrant. We would lay in bed on Saturday morning and instead of me reviewing medical charts he would pack our bags and we'd head to the beach, lazily drink wine all afternoon in the warm sun with our feet in the sand and our hearts on fire. Then, we'd find a nice hotel and make love all night. Sunday we would sleep until whenever, call in room service and make love all day. I was deliriously in love with life, maybe even Daryl too, but I was feeling so alive—so wanton and wanted. It was a crazy time. I know you may not want to hear this but please try to understand."

"I am, Anita. I am hearing you. I'm listening."

"After Mom died, I felt cloudy all the time. It was as if my energy was floating around my body, not in it. I felt reborn with Daryl, at first." She hesitated. "Barbara, it was really good for a few months, and I felt rebellious and alive and free of all the restrictions of my life as a doctor. I hope you can understand. I noticed that Daryl got out of control when he drank, even in the early weeks, but he didn't take out his rage on me, at first. I don't think he had much ammunition on me, but after we married the barbs started coming. I was shocked and tried to reason with him—reassure him, but that didn't help."

She turned to Barbara. "Have you ever tried to reason with a drunk? It's like reasoning with a two-year-old. Anyway, now I'm here with a broken hand, a patched up eye, double vision and a broken spirit. What I would do for some semblance of normal again to not have lived through these last months with Daryl."

Barbara spoke softly. "I get it Anita. I get that you needed to be rebellious and why. I get the hurt too." She wrapped her arms around her and hugged her gently. "I do get it, my friend. I'm sorry you're hurting so much. You have me. You have Thomas. We are here for you. I can't tell you that enough. I do understand."

She hugged her tighter. *More than you'll ever know. I understand. I, too, have a secret, a deep secret, one I have not shared with anyone.*

TWENTY-THREE

That night as Barbara lay down to sleep, she didn't dream of her wonderful husband as she did during her nap. Instead she dreamt about her secret.

My secret, buried in the murky, cavernous part of my brain only surfaced after Anita's bruised face reminded me of it. I never told my mother, Bobby, or even Thomas. I have never told anyone.

I still remember the creaky, drafty farmhouse that I lived in as a young child and the coarse, parched lawn that my younger brother, Bobby and I romped on, wrestling and giggling until supper time. I had a mop of Shirley Temple-like, curly russet hair. Bobby had a straight golden bleached mane; both of our skin bronzed and delicate, innocent. The crackling, weather worn, faded gray farm dwelling with its moaning wraparound porch was what we called home. It was seven miles from town on bumpy, potholed roads. Bobby and I were each other's sole company and best friends. He was four years younger than me. I was his protector and big sister.

It was a scorching, sticky July night. I was about seven years old. My parents often had loud arguments, but this particular screaming match escalated to thunderous banging of doors and cursing, slurred words. Bobby, who slept in the same small bedroom as I, just down the hall from the commotion in the living room, woke and started to cry. The fighting was not unusual, but the pitch of the screams from my mom was more primal than normal. We could hear my dad slapping my mom. She pleaded with him to stop and be quiet so as not to wake us, but it was too late.

Bobby crept into my bed, sobbing. Together, we made a makeshift tent with my faded, threadbare quilt. I sang him songs, trying to distract him from the uproar down the hall. I tenderly rubbed his back singing, *Jesus loves me, this I know, for the Bible tells me so,* until he was asleep, or so I thought.

As the screaming intensified, I got more scared. I snuck out of bed. In my bare feet, with the frayed hem of my lace, pink princess nightgown dragging on the floor, I tiptoed down the hall and peeked around the corner into the living room. I saw my angry, scruffy, and sweaty dad slap my mom cruelly across her face. Her head tilted sideways awkwardly. Her tangled, blonde hair flew into her face. Her arms and hands instinctively came up, protecting herself; a boxer's stance, guarding her from further blows. She screamed at him. I was too afraid to reveal myself. Mom turned and left down the hall. Then, out of the corner of my eye, I saw Bobby. I thought he was asleep. *Bobby, what are you doing out of bed? What are you going to do? Please, get away from Dad.*

Clad in his worn, footed pajamas with his big toes sticking out, he was crying in front of my dad yelling at him. "Daddy, no hurt Mommy. Daddy, Daddy, no . . ." With his tiny, clenched fists Bobby started pounding on my dad's burly, bare chest while he lay slumped in his drunken stupor on the couch. Then, my dad, like a grizzly disturbed from hibernation, barreled off the couch and with the back of his hand whacked my baby brother. He flew across the room tumbling like a rag doll, yelping.

My dad bellowed at him, "Go back to bed. Stop sniveling like a snot-nosed sissy."

Stunned, little Bobby scurried to his feet and ran down the hall. Bile rumbled in my throat. I had to do something to finally stop my dad. *I have to protect Bobby. I have to protect Mommy too.* My dad teeter-tottered back to the couch and flopped down, slumped into it, eyes closed. I quietly sprinted to kitchen, my feet gliding, skimming the floor. I scanned the kitchen for something, anything to protect us. I nearly dropped the heavy cast iron skillet as I pulled it down from the stove. With both hands tightly clasped around the rough, hard handle, I stepped catlike, back to the living room. The only thing sticking above the back of the couch was my dad's balding crown, but that's all I needed as a target. With the might of a mamma bear protecting her cub, I swung the heavy skillet like a baseball bat into the back of my dad's head. Thud. The vibrations ricocheted down my arms.

My dad yelled, tried to turn and stand but tripped on his muddied boots lying on the floor next to the couch. He fell clumsily forward and banged his head on the corner of the coffee table, collapsing to the rag rug on the cracked linoleum floor. One hand covered his head, but I could see the scarlet blood seeping between his fingers. I gasped for air and scampered into my bedroom, gripping the weighty frying pan so tightly my clenched hands had turned blue. Hastily, I shoved the pan under the bed and catapulted up onto the lumpy mattress. Bobby was in his own bed, whimpering, and his covers over his head. With wildly trembling hands, I pulled my tatty quilt over me—my protective tent. My heart thumped against my hardened chest. I couldn't pull any air down into my cemented lungs. I rounded my tiny body into a fetal position, and in the slightest whisper breath I uttered, "What have I just done?"

Oceans of tears, pent up from months of restraint, flowed down my cheeks. Bobby snuck out of his bed and peeked under my quilt. I nodded and he scurried up and into my arms. We huddled together, crouched like two frightened wild baby animals; afraid ... of what would happen next. Then I sang, in halting breaths, *Jesus loves me this I know ... for the Bible ... tells me so ...*

Sometime in the fierce darkness I was startled by husky, melodic snores coming from down the hall. I gingerly slid out of bed, sleepy eyed, careful not to disturb Bobby. I crouched under the bed and tugged at the heavy skillet, bringing it to my grip. With my defense weapon tightly seized, I crept down the hall, my small feet against the floor, inaudible. I saw my dad on the yellowing linoleum in an awkward position. Dried blood was matted on his hair and ears. Repugnant snoring spouted from his ugly, angry face. I was relieved by his snores, knowing I hadn't killed him.

I snuck into the kitchen and heaved the hefty pan back onto the stove. No one would know. Bobby didn't see me. Mom didn't see me and neither did Dad. Holding my breath, I tip-toed gingerly back down the hall, this time taking two small steps in the direction of my sleeping father. His snores were furious and scary. Dried crusty brown blood was caked between his fingers. I could see a small round stain on the floor near his head but he was alive. I shuffled back to bed listening to his defiant snores.

With the first hint of morning light, the rooster's crowing wakened me. I walked slowly into the living room. Dad was not there. In his place was the thin, fidgeting frame of my mom, in her torn nightgown, kneeling down near a bucket, scrubbing the blood stained floor. She glanced up at me. Her eyes were bloodshot and swollen. Her cheeks already discolored blue.

She softly said to me, "Your dad fell last night. He's in bed now. I'm just cleaning up. Is Bobby awake?"

"No. Did Dad say what happened?"

Dismissively, she said, "It's no concern of yours. Go into the kitchen and get yourself some cereal. I'll be there in a minute."

Dad stayed in his bedroom for what seemed like weeks. I knew that he didn't know what hit him or who. For the next six weeks, I watched as dad walked around punch drunk, staggering; his speech slurred but not from alcohol this time. He was never quite the same. The scar on his head was thick and uneven; his personality flat; his voice monotone. There were no more fights, but there was no affection either. He never went to the bar again.

Bobby and I played quiet games in our room, both afraid that we might wake up the sleeping demon in my dad. Neither of us spoke about that night. The house was still, the air stagnant. At that time I thought I broke my father, my family, but I know now that the family was broken long before that scorching summer night.

Then, one crisp fall day, before dawn, my dad left to work in the fields. He never came back.

Apparently, his tractor skidded and tipped over on the icy road, pinning him; killing him. Although we grieved, there was a sense of relief, a release. We were out of danger. My father's terror buried.

To this day, I wonder if I had something to do with my dad's death. I have lived with the secret of that blistering night and the skillet, all my life.

Mom had to go to work to support us after dad died. She worked in town in the medical office of Dr. Art Spelling, a family practitioner. Two years later, Mom married him and our lives changed significantly. We moved to town into an enormous, rambling house with green grass, not that parched lawn from the farm. Bobby and I were still best buddies, and we gained a new big brother, Jacob, Art's son. He was four years older than me and serious, but the three of us quickly became friends. We had friends in town who invited us to parties and sleepovers. We were finally accepted in the community. The biggest difference was in my mom. She sang while cleaning the big house. She made cakes and cookies. She wore clean, pretty, flowery dresses every day. Color returned to her face; she blushed and glowed. My new dad adopted us. I had a real father and, more importantly, I had a valid example of what love for a wife and family should be; supportive, respectful, kind, and loving. Thomas Kirkland reminds me of Art.

WAKING WITH A JOLT AND TRYING TO SHAKE OFF the dream of her childhood with her biological father, Barbara put on her slippers and quietly padded into the kitchen. There she warmed herself a glass of milk, a remedy from her mother that they both used to help them sleep. She thought of Art, the father who adopted her, whom she respected, and her happy childhood in his care. She thought of life with Thomas, a gentle, loving husband. After she drank the warm milk she set the glass down and turned her focus on Anita. *I know that Anita will find her Thomas too, but first she needs to get out of the threat of danger and away from the nightmare of Daryl for good.*

TWENTY-FOUR

WHILE ANITA WAS RECOVERING AT THE KIRKLAND'S beach house, Daryl was stewing in his office in a frustrated, dark mood after a two-martini lunch. He ran his manicured, bulky hands through his thick hair then picked up the phone. *That bitch. She's not going to get the best of me. Those goody-goody, high and mighty Kirklands know where she is. I know it. I'll hire Bill Cratelli to find her.* His hand reached deep in his pocket where he found the hard handle of his pistol.

"Bill Cratelli, Private Investigations."

"Bill, its Daryl."

"Daryl who?"

"For Christ's sakes, Bill, you know damn well who I am. I paid you a small fortune to investigate my wife, Anita. Now do you remember me?"

"Yes, Daryl, now I remember. What can I do for you?"

Flustered, Daryl spit out, "Bill, I need your help again."

"What is it this time? I already did a thorough investigation on your wife a few months ago, and she's squeaky clean. She isn't seeing anyone else, Daryl." His voice grew irritated.

"You said that but I'm not convinced because of this new development." Daryl's words came out sloppy. Cratelli could hear the slurring in his voice as though he was drunk or on something. "Anyway, she's gone now and I want you to find my bitch wife," Daryl demanded. "She's missing."

"Daryl, there's no reason to swear. What do you mean she's missing?"

With his voice raised Daryl said, "Yes, damn it. She's missing. That's what I just said." He banged his fist on the desk.

Cratelli said, "Daryl, you're going to have to give me more information than that."

Angrily, he spit out, "I need you to find my bitch of a wife, Dr. Goody-Two-Shoes."

"What do you mean find her?"

"It's like this. We had an argument last Friday night and she's been gone since then. She's not at her practice. She doesn't answer her cell phone."

"Have you called the police?"

"No, no. She's just avoiding me. Her office said she had an out of town emergency and won't tell me when she's coming back or offer any information. I'm sure they know more—know where she is—but they won't tell me. She's my wife, damn it."

"Wait, Daryl. You need to calm down so I can understand exactly what you need from me. Can you come into the office and explain what this is all about so I can get more details?"

Indignantly, Daryl answered, "What more do you want? I told you Anita is missing."

"Calm down, Daryl. If you want my help I'll need more information than 'she's missing.'" He continued, "Like I said, you need to come in if you want me to explore taking this case. I'm available today after three."

Daryl spewed, "I can get there at four but no sooner."

"That works. I'll see you in the office."

Daryl slammed the receiver down.

CRATELLI PUT THE PHONE DOWN, SHOOK HIS HEAD, and spun around in his chair toward his Cherrywood bookcase filled with legal books. He opened the top drawer of his desk. His hand gun was safely lying under some papers. The hairs on the back of his neck stiffened. *I'm sure there is a whole lot more to this story. I didn't like this guy when I first did the investigation on Dr. Stone. He said he was absolutely sure she was having an affair but I found her to be squeaky clean. There was no evidence she was so much as having an extra glass of wine at medical conferences.* He picked up the heavy crystal paperweight on his desk turning it over in his hand. It was etched with evenly balanced scales, the symbol of justice.

Daryl was a pain in the ass during the last investigation. He questioned my approach to the investigation from the very beginning.

This guy is paranoid, suspicious at best. I know this type. They can be dangerous and abusive. Explode at any time like a bomb going off. This doesn't sound good. I wonder if he had anything to do with her disappearance. I knew I didn't like this guy. There's certainly more to this story. I don't have a good feeling about this. I need to see what's really going on. This story isn't adding up. What a condescending jerk. I don't really think I want to get involved with this case but something tells me Dr. Stone may be in danger, grave danger.

Unable to concentrate of the file in front of him he stood up, pulled the gun out of the drawer and tucked it in his underarm holster. He walked out of his office, locking the front door behind him and inhaled the crisp fall air.

Cratelli returned after a brisk walk and managed to get some work done. He wasn't looking forward to his meeting with Daryl.

DARYL ARRIVED PROMPTLY AT 4 P.M. HE SAT IN THE high-backed chair facing Cratelli.

"Okay, Daryl. Tell me a little bit more than your wife is missing. Where do you think she's gone? When did she leave? Did she leave a note? You said you didn't call the police, why not?"

Daryl fidgeted in the chair, shaking his head back

and forth. "I don't know where she is or why she left."

Cratelli raised his eyebrows and rolled his eyes.

"You have to give me more than that if you want me to help you."

"We had a disagreement and she left in the middle of the night."

"Okay, what night?"

Getting answers from Daryl was like pulling hundred-year old weeds from the Sahara Desert but eventually Cratelli got enough information from Daryl. Reluctantly he decided to take the case and Daryl left his office.

CRATELLI WASN'T SURE HOW HE WOULD HANDLE IT IF he found Dr. Stone. Daryl was a real piece of work. He was a challenge last time because he doubted Cratelli's conclusion that she was not involved with any other man but he paid his huge bill. This time, after his conversation with Daryl, he was very concerned about Dr. Stone and her safety. He took a deep breath, chomped on his pen, and scribbled down a note, Watch Daryl.

After Daryl left, Cratelli picked up the phone and called attorney John Osborn. His office was closed. He left a message saying that Daryl Davidson had contacted him trying to find his wife, Dr. Anita Stone.

TWENTY-FIVE

B ILL CRATELLI SAT DOWN IN HIS OFFICE, TOOK A
sip of his cappuccino and listened to his one
voice mail. It was from John Osborn, Anita's attorney
with whom Cratelli had worked with on a couple of
domestic abuse cases. Immediately, when Cratelli
heard Daryl's name, the back of neck prickled hot and
sweat beaded on his forehead.

Cratelli listened to the message again. John said
that there was a temporary restraining order out on
Daryl. He had beaten Anita up and this wasn't the
first time. When Cratelli first took the case he
checked for legal actions against Daryl, but the
restraining order had not been processed and wasn't
in the system.

He chastised himself. *Why didn't I listen to my
instincts when Daryl called about Dr. Stone being missing?*

Thank God I didn't have any information yet. I knew something was terribly wrong with this whole picture. His stomach tightened and violently rumbled. His half-digested morning bagel churned and soured. *I knew it. Daryl has something to do with her being gone.* He slapped the desk. *I wonder if she's okay. I wonder if she's even still alive.* He shook his head back and forth. *Daryl seems anxious to find her. I don't think she's dead. She must be in hiding.*

Cratelli called John for more details and then, trying to stifle his nausea, dialed Daryl's number. He picked up on the second ring.

"Hello."

"Daryl, its Bill Cratelli. I want to speak with you about—"

Daryl interrupted before Cratelli could say anything further. He stiffened his back, "Did you find my wife?"

Cratelli snapped into the phone. "No, Daryl. I didn't find her and you shouldn't either. There is a restraining order on you to stay away from her."

"Oh that … well."

"Wait, Daryl." Cratelli's voice got louder and he had to calm himself before continuing. He took a quick breath and rolled his shoulders. "I take restraining orders very seriously and you should too. You have been ordered by the courts to stay away from Dr. Stone. This is nothing to sneeze about. Do you want to end up in jail? You haven't been forthcoming with me about all the facts."

A cocky-sounding defiant Daryl said, "Oh that."

"That is a big deal and I suggest you obey it. I will not be working your case. Again, this is serious business, Daryl, and you need to stay away from Dr. Stone."

Cratelli heard the phone slam.

He placed the phone back in its cradle and ran his hands through his salt and pepper hair. *I'm going to find you Anita. Somebody needs to warn you about this guy. He seems dangerous. I know these types. He gives me the creeps.*

DARYL PACED THE FLOOR AND RUBBED HIS FOREHEAD. *Screw you Cratelli. You're not the only game in town. I'm sure I can find someone to help me. I'll find my wife. Till death do us part, right? Where are you Anita? Why won't you talk to me?* He put his hand to his chin; the thinker. *Where did you go? Why aren't you in your office? You never miss work. I've got an idea.*

He picked up the phone and dialed a different private investigator who agreed to take the case.

TWENTY-SIX

AFTER A COUPLE DAYS THOMAS DECIDED HE would be more comfortable spending time with his ladies at the beach. He left his medical office late in the afternoon anticipating the surprise. He had a bounce in his step. His overnight bag was neatly packed and stored in the trunk of his car. The angle of the sun on the leafy Pistache trees surrounding the parking lot formed lengthy, seductive shadows. The air was fresh and still, light and clean, as was his mood. The work week, although tiring and busy from taking on Anita's patient load and surgeries, had flown by.

Susan, the office manager who was a public relations genius, had expertly handled Anita's patients' questions about her absence, spinning a tale about an out-of-town family emergency with just the right amount of concern and compassion while still keeping Anita's situation under wraps. No one really got any specific details about what type of emergency it was or what family member was involved but after Susan's story, Anita's patients were very under-standing.

The one call that had disturbed her was from Daryl. He had repeatedly probed her for answers about Anita's whereabouts, but Susan kept her composure and gave him no information.

Susan was a priceless employee who had not only juggled the patient schedule and staff but managed to fulfill Thomas's requests to pick up some Sunflowers —Barbara's favorite fall flower—and a nice bottle of chardonnay. She rescheduled Friday patients so Thomas could get out of the office early to head to the Pajaro Dunes beach house.

Thomas was very much looking forward to spending time with Barbara and Anita at the beach house. Although he spoke nightly with his wife, he missed her. When they were much younger, he had various medical conferences to attend which took him away for days at a time, but now that they were in their later years, he rarely spent a night apart from her. He enjoyed their time together, especially now that he was semi-retired. He looked forward to their casual uninterrupted dinners now that he was rarely on call. He was also excited about greater participation with Barbara in their charity work for under privileged youth.

Thomas had received no more late night visits or

calls from Daryl since Monday night, but he was concerned that Daryl was brewing something up. Susan told him that he had called the office seeking information. *I wonder what he's been up to the last four days.*

He hoped that Anita would be strong enough to leave Daryl for good. Susan told Thomas that Daryl had moved out of the house, or at least most of his clothes were gone. Anita's restraining order was in place, but he didn't actually believe that Daryl would just walk away that easily. Thomas hoped that Daryl had cooled down and that Anita could work with John Osborn without fear to get things in order and start the divorce proceedings.

Thomas could hardly wait to see his wife's face when he surprised her later today. He started his gray Mercedes and pushed the window control buttons, rolling down the windows. He inhaled the soft fragrant scent of jasmine surrounding the parking lot. There were still several cars parked in the medical complex as Thomas pulled onto the street. His shoulders eased and a smile lit his face as he thought of his plan to surprise the ladies with flowers and wine and join in on some of those late night popcorn/chardonnay conversations. He hadn't surprised Barbara in a very long time, nor was he known for being spontaneous, out of character for a dedicated, sensible orthopedic surgeon.

On the drive, Barbara's voice echoed in his mind, "I've watched Anita's eye swelling recede and the kaleidoscope of colors from her bruises transform from ugly plum purple to jaundice. It looks more like a bullseye now—not that I'm suggesting anyone ever take a punch at her again—but she definitely has a target around her eye. The cast on her right arm is the most prominent reminder of the thrashing Daryl gave her a week ago, but the internal scars and fears go much deeper."

She told Thomas about how she and Anita sat for hours in their pajamas on Barbara's bed over late night popcorn and chardonnay. He really missed his wife.

"So, Anita's body is healing?" he had asked Barbara last night.

"Yes, very much so."

"How's her vision?"

"She said it hasn't gotten any worse. I don't think she's straining her eyes, maybe her brain but not her eyes. We haven't even turned on the TV. We've really bonded this week. We chat about nothing and everything," she told Thomas.

"How are you doing, sweetheart? Are you holding up okay? Do you miss me as much as I miss you?" he teased.

"Yes, of course I miss you. On a much lighter note, however, my feet are silky smooth now. The sand is better than any pumice stone. I'll have no more complaining from you about my rough, cold feet startling you in bed. Well, I'm sure they are still cold but they are not rough anymore." She continued, "We've walked for hours daily on the beach. Some days it's cool, and I have to bundle up but we get our walks in. Other days the sun is brilliant in the sky and warm. Ah, October in California."

"Does this mean you've given up your pedicures?"

"Don't be silly Thomas. Not unless you're going to be painting my toenails every other week."

He laughed. "No."

"Okay then."

That was the extent of their conversation last night. Tonight he would be able to snuggle next to his wife and those silky feet she had been talking about.

Thomas needed to stop for gas. That's when he sighted the 1995 Sapphire Blue Ford GT Mustang. It reminded him of the 1966 Blue Metallic Mustang he bought after completing his fifth year of private practice. *That's the second time I've seen one of those cars today. The first time was in the parking lot at work.*

What a classy-looking car. Maybe I should get me one for old times sake—bring back my youthful days. Barbara and I sure had a lot of fun in the old '66. It could reignite the fire of our youth.

After getting gas, he headed back on the road and turned onto the on-ramp of the freeway still reminiscing about the early, romantic, steamy years with Barbara. He sang with abandon, along with Ray Stevens on the oldies station, "Everything is beautiful in its own way ... like a starry summer night ..."

His posture straightened taller while the muscles in his shoulder relaxed; carefree, the plan of checking out a new Mustang, the upbeat music, the anticipation of sea breezes, the grainy sand and his wife lying next to him.

He glanced in his rearview mirror. *Uh. That's the Mustang from the gas station behind me. That seems a little odd. I'm just lollygagging down the highway in the slow lane, taking my time. Someone in that fast car should be way past me by now.*

That's when the hairs on the back of his neck stood up. Goosebumps erupted on his arms. His neck tightened. Hard knots formed in his shoulder blades. *That is the same car that was in the parking lot at the office and again at the gas station. Am I being followed? Is it Daryl? No, I don't think so. He has a Porsche. Oh my god. What do I do? Calm down, Thomas.*

He took a cleansing breath and slowed his breathing. Consciously he relaxed his neck. He was used to dealing with emergencies in the Emergency Room but not on the road. He loosened his iron grip from the steering wheel.

He changed lanes and slowed down but the Mustang still didn't pass him. *If I'm being followed I can't go to the beach house. I don't want to bring trouble there. Daryl must be looking for Anita or he's hired someone to find her. So, what do I do now?*

He took the next exit off the freeway. The Mustang followed. *Think fast, Thomas. Think fast. Go to a public place. Don't be alone. Nothing will happen to you in a public place.*

He spotted a restaurant with a few cars in the

parking lot—Giovanni's Italian Restaurant. *I'm glad some Italians eat early.* He got out of his car and hurried into the restaurant. It was small and dark with old brick walls. It took a minute for his eyes to adjust to the darkness. There were white tablecloths on the tiny tables surrounded by chocolate-colored chairs. There was antique bar over on the right side which sat about six. A silver-haired couple was seated near the back of the restaurant at one of the tables for four. Thomas rushed up to the couple.

He plopped down in one of the empty chairs at the table. His words came out like a steamroller. "This is going to sound very odd but please listen to me. My name is Dr. Thomas Kirkland. I'm an orthopedic surgeon practicing at Washington Hospital in Fremont. I think I'm being followed. Please act like you know me, that I'm here to meet you."

The couple stared at Thomas. Sweat beaded on his forehead.

"I can show you my hospital identification soon, but I'm no criminal or anything."

The elderly couple looked perplexed by their new dinner intruder. The woman, primly dressed in a smart looking navy blue pants suit, shrugged her shoulders. The man nodded. Thomas sank in the chair facing the rustic, wooden front door.

A clean-shaven man with neatly trimmed black hair, khaki pants and short sleeved shirt sauntered in. He was holding a newspaper.

TWENTY-SEVEN

IT'S NOT DARYL, THOUGHT THOMAS WITH RELIEF.
Instead, it was a man with dark sideburns. His
tense shoulders and straight upright posture looked
military. Daryl, on the other hand, was much younger
and didn't have any sideburns. He had a much more
laissez-faire, cool guy presence; polar opposites from
Mr. Mysterious with a newspaper now standing by the
bar.

The elderly man, with whom Thomas was now
sitting, turned to him and scanned his face as if it
would reveal what was happening, "Is this for real?
Are you really a doctor? Doctors usually aren't known
for getting followed around." He drew his shoulders
back and looked directly into Thomas's eyes, "We're
regulars here and I'm calling over the owner,
Giovanni, right now so don't do anything funny."

Thomas shifted his eyes toward the newspaper man. "I think that might be the guy following me." Thomas leaned in toward the elderly man. "Go ahead. Call the owner over. That's a great idea. Introduce me to him."

Puzzled, the man questioned, "Introduce you? I don't even know you."

Lily, the neatly coiffed lady sitting at the table, her pearl earrings shimmering softly on her ears, turned to her husband. "Come on Michael. That guy at the bar definitely looks suspicious. You almost wonder where his trench coat is. And, he has a newspaper in his hand." She leaned in and whispered, "No regular guy walks around with a newspaper in his hands," she whispered, "unless he's going into the bathroom."

Michael picked up his black leather-bound menu, hunched down a bit, and peered over the top. "You're right, Lily. Look, he's turned sideways on the bar stool so he can watch the entire restaurant. That's odd."

"I can tell he's a private eye."

"What, Lily? How can you tell? I think you've been watching too many Colombo reruns."

"Look, he brought in the newspaper but isn't even reading it. Why would he do that? Why is he just sitting there looking around the restaurant? It's not like this is a pick-up joint." She turned to Thomas softening her face, "You are a doctor aren't you?"

Thomas nodded and spoke gently, "Yes, and I

know this sounds crazy. It's not something I had expected in my lifetime either. I wasn't trained for this in medical school but please listen. A colleague of mine, actually my business partner, was beaten up by her husband. She has a restraining order against him and she's hiding. He thinks I know where she is. I think that's why this guy is following me."

The lines in Lily's brow smoothed. "You do seem like a nice guy, maybe even a doctor, but how do we know you're telling us the truth and you're not some criminal hiding from the police? I've seen that on Colombo too."

"I'll show you my hospital I.D. but I can't right now. That will look too weird. I want to throw this guy off my trail so here's my plan." He used his hands for effect. "If you pretend you know me and we're here to meet for dinner, I think this guy will be satisfied that I'm not meeting my partner and may go away."

Mr. Mysterious swirled the lime with his cocktail straw, but he still sat sideways to the bar. He scanned the room.

Thomas kinked his neck, releasing tension. "I've got it. Here's my office number. Talk with Susan, my office manager. She knows where I am. Is there a pay phone here? I just have a pager. My partner has been bugging me to turn it in for a cellular phone, but they are so big and bulky. I've been waiting for a newer, sleeker model."

Lily said, "Yes. Phones are by the restrooms."

"Okay, call and talk with Susan or Elizabeth from the answering service. They will answer anything you want to know. Describe me to them. They'll verify who I am." Thomas lifted his eyebrows and gestured with his hands, "I'll buy you dinner. Will you help me?"

Michael peered at Thomas "Shouldn't we just call the police?"

Lily answered for him. "I don't know what we'd tell them."

"I know. It's not like the guy has done anything to us," Thomas said. "I just want to get out of here, away from him."

Lily repeated the office phone number and got up from the table. After smoothing her sharply creased pants with her delicate age-spotted hands, she headed toward the bathroom.

Michael gently clasped Lily's hand. "Sit down, Lily."

Thomas looked confused. "I know this is awkward for you, but I don't know what else to do. I really am Dr. Thomas Kirkland, an orthopedic surgeon."

Michael asked, "Can you give me the names of a few of the internists who practice at the hospital?"

"I know Dr. Adam Rogers and Dr. Dan Malcolm."

"Yes, okay."

Lily nervously scanned the room, her glasses just peeking above the menu. "Wow, our own personal

Colombo here at Giovanni's Restaurant."

Michael turned to Lily and chided, "Stop the talk about Colombo. Let's figure out what to do now. I believe Dr. Kirkland is who he says he is."

Thomas said, "Thank you." He sighed. "Now I just have to figure out how to get out of here without that guy following me, unless, of course, the two of you want to have dinner with a stranger. That would really throw the guy off."

"I have an idea," Michael said. "There's a back door in the kitchen. I could have Giovanni take the two of us on a kitchen tour. We've done that before. Like I said, we're regulars. We've been coming here for a good ten years."

"That's a good plan, Michael." Lily turned to Thomas and whispered, "You could sneak out the back door. I'll stay here and watch the guy for you." She smiled and softly said, "I'll trip him if he gets up to follow."

Michael turned to Lily. "You would be willing to do that, trip a guy? This is a side of you I've never seen."

"Just helping out a fellow doctor."

Thomas tilted his head and turned toward Michael. "You're a doctor?"

"Yes, I'm Dr. Michael Johnson, a retired internist just enjoying the good life with the Mrs." He reached for Lily's hand. "It's our forty-sixth anniversary today. Lily and I were expecting a quiet early dinner at our favorite neighborhood restaurant, not taking part in our sleepy town's own version of Perry Mason. This will certainly be something to tell our kids and grandkids." He gestured for the waiter. "Let's see if Giovanni can help us out."

"Thanks, Dr. Johnson. Thanks Lily. Happy Anniversary. Not the quiet meal you had planned is it?"

With Giovanni in on the plan, Thomas and Michael headed back to the kitchen. Giovanni, in his gregarious Italian voice said, "Sure, I'll give you a little kitchen tour. It will just take a couple minutes."

Lily remained seated. She spoke loud enough for Mr. Mysterious to hear her, as well as the other couple sitting at the bar. "You go ahead. I've seen it before. I'm still trying to decide what to have for dinner." She signaled for Michael to lean down close to her. She whispered, "Tell Dr. Kirkland to get the guy's license plate number. That's what Colombo would tell him to do—get the license plate number."

Exasperated he replied, "Okay. Okay."

Mr. Mysterious stayed at the bar and slowly sipped his drink. Giovanni lead the way to the kitchen, talking with his hands and speaking in his exaggerated, thick Italian accent. Once in the kitchen, Thomas thanked Dr. Johnson and Giovanni, then slipped out the back door and got into his car. He drove around the side where he found the parked Mustang. He memorized the license plate number and then sped out of the parking lot and down the road. His eyes stayed glued to his rearview mirror. No headlights followed him. When he came to the on-ramp, he had to decide. Should he head back home or continue with his plan to meet up with Barbara and Anita at the beach house?

Thomas veered onto the freeway heading back home. He didn't want to put Barbara or Anita in any kind of danger. *I'll call John when I get home and ask for his advice.*

He gazed down at the neatly wrapped flowers in the front seat. *I'll put the flowers in a vase of water on the counter. The wine, maybe I'll drink that myself. I'm not on call.* He contemplated whether he should tell Barbara he was being followed. *Maybe, maybe not.*

After several miles his face finally relaxed, his hands eased. The blood flowed freely back to his scrubbed fingernails. No distinct headlights followed him.

On the curvy dark road his mind wandered back to when he was fourteen and the car crash.

HIS DAD MUST HAVE WORN TOO MUCH OLD SPICE the night before the accident when he and Thomas's mom went to the movies. Thomas could still smell a faint hint of it inside their 1946 Buick station wagon. His four-year-old sister, Annie, with her wispy blond hair covering her chubby cheeks, sat in the middle of the back seat between Audrey and him. Audrey was his ten-year-old sister. Thomas was excited to finally be growing into a man. A sliver of a mustache had erupted on his upper lip almost overnight. His dad had noticed. When they got into the car that late morning after church for a Sunday drive, his dad had suggested that the men sit on one side of the car while the girls sit on the other. It was the first time he had referred to Thomas as a man. Proudly, he took his place in the back seat behind his dad. *When I become a man I'm not wearing Old Spice. I can't stand that woodsy, spicy smell.*

Thomas's mom was in the front seat. It was stuffy and hot in the car, so Thomas rolled down his window part way and stuck out his hand cupping the wind. The air was only slightly cooler outside the car, but it helped dissipate the smell of his dad's after shave.

Annie was barely awake, her eyes tiny slits. It was getting close to her nap time. She leaned down resting her head on Thomas's lap. Audrey and Thomas were poking each other in the shoulders behind Annie just trying to annoy one another. "Got you," Thomas pronounced as he poked his sister then quickly returned his arm to his side.

"Got you back. Ha-ha-ha," she said.

"Stop it."

"You started it." Poke, poke.

"Quit touching me."

Their mom turned around in the front seat, "Shush, you two. Let Annie sleep."

Suddenly, there was an angry loud screech from their car's tires as the five of them lunged forward.

His dad was braking to avoid hitting a car that had unexpectedly stopped in front of them. Thomas remembered hitting his head and holding tightly onto Annie's small body so that she wouldn't fall onto the floor of the car. When the car finally stopped and they were resting back into their seats there was a deafening, jet-loud noise and a jolting metal crash as the car behind them rammed into the back of their car. Again, they all jerked forward and back again. Then, came yet another crashing blast as they smashed into the car in front of them; the one they had previously avoided.

Their station wagon was sandwiched between the two cars now. The crash happened in a matter of seconds but each detail was still etched in Thomas's brain. He remembered the violent jostling back and forth with each collision. It felt like his brain was rumbling around in his skull. His eyes were blurry. A warm trickle of blood pooled in the corner of his eye then ran down his cheek. He tried to lift his right arm to wipe off the blood, but the right side of his body was awkwardly twisted and stuck between the front and back car seats. Audrey was crying and Annie was screaming, "My arm. My arm!"

Annie's petite right arm had gotten twisted and crunched between him and the back seat. There was blood on the side of her body. One of her bones in her lower arm had snapped and was poking through her skin. It was jagged and uneven. Thomas was shaking. Annie was sobbing, "Mommy. Mommy, what happened? My arm." Annie's voice was jerky and weak, barely audible. Her words came out in bits and spurts. "It's bleeding. I can't move it." Annie voice was raw; her breath rough. Thomas didn't know what to do. He couldn't free her because their arms were wrenched together between the seats and each other. He took his left hand and stroked Annie's forehead. His mom turned around glassy-eyed and dazed. She tried to open her car door but it was jammed. Thomas remembered the guttural moans coming from his mom in front seat.

Somehow his dad got out of the car. He tried to open the back door where Thomas was sitting but it wouldn't budge. He raced around to the back door where Audrey was and tugged it open. She tumbled out of the back seat. When his dad saw Annie's arm and dress covered in blood he catapulted into the back seat where Audrey had been. He scooted as close to Annie as he could and bent his long legs up in a ball. Thomas remembered the superman force his dad used as he shoved the front seat forward just enough to release the pressure on the two of them. He scooped Annie up, gingerly supporting her broken arm in his strong ones and got her out of the car. Thomas followed. Audrey was standing near the car, shivering and confused. His mother was frantically banging, thudding her shoulder on her door but it was jammed shut.

While bundling Annie in his arms, Thomas's dad instructed the other two kids to follow him to a tree about twenty feet away. "Sit here, in the shade," he directed them. He was still holding Annie as she whimpered into his shirt, moaning and shaking. Dad placed her into Thomas arms. He ripped off his Sunday dress shirt, buttons flying on the pavement. Thomas couldn't believe his super-hero strength. Blood was running down Annie's arm. There was blood coming from Thomas's head mingling with Annie's. Her Sunday best dress was smeared with their combined blood. It had a metallic smell to it. He had never noticed the smell of blood before.

His father lovingly took Annie's arm. She winced in pain as he skillfully maneuvered the bone back into alignment and wrapped it with the torn sleeve of his Old Spice scented shirt. Then, he took Thomas's adolescent hands into his mighty ones and placed them on Annie's wrapped arm. With an authoritative voice he said, "Hold onto her arm, apply pressure. Do not let it move. We need to stop the bleeding. Do you understand?" His eyes were laser beams pointed intently at teenage Thomas.

Thomas felt the immense responsibility of his sister. "Yes, Dad," he said.

The shirt around Annie's arm soon became soaked in crimson blood. Thomas remembered holding her and praying that she would be okay. His dad looked at his son's bleeding head, a deep gash near his right eye. He tore off another piece of his shirt and wrapped it around Thomas's head. "You'll be fine. Your job is to take care of Annie."

Hissing. Thomas remembered the distinct hissing. His dad turned to the mangled car knowing that his wife was still trapped inside. "I've got to get Mom out of the car," he said. Thomas would never forget the steely look in his dad's eyes as he said to Thomas. "You're in charge now." His dad sprinted back to the car leaving Thomas with his siblings sitting on the ground.

The car was leaking gas. That didn't stop Thomas's dad from racing toward it to retrieve his wife.

Strangers came up to Thomas but he didn't understand them. He couldn't focus on words, only on his primary responsibility, Annie and Audrey. He did remember an old man with a bloody shirt mumbling, "I'm sorry. Are you kids okay?"

When Thomas's dad reached the car he crawled in the driver's side door. Somehow he got his wife out. Her foot was flopping in an awkward direction as he and another man helped her limp to Thomas and his sisters. His mom sat down and took Annie from Thomas, into her arms but he never let go of Annie's arm. He remembered his mother's soothing lullaby-voice as she sang to Annie and rocked her. His dad picked up Audrey, who was shivering, and held her to keep her warm. Then, there was a deafening explosion as their car burst into flames. The Kirkland family turned toward the burning car.

It was Thomas's dad's quick thinking, expertise in critical situations and the training he had received as an Army medic that saved their lives that day. His dad never talked about the war. His mom had told Thomas that he was a decorated war hero. He was Thomas's hero too.

Thomas ended up with a concussion and a few stitches in his forehead but recovered quickly. Audrey was shaken up but had no visible injuries, nor did their dad. Thomas's mom needed surgery on her ankle to repair her injuries. Annie lost a lot of blood and needed a transfusion. She also underwent surgery to repair her broken arm with screws. Three months later she was playing on the monkey bars as if the accident never happened and, proudly, showing off her scar.

That fateful Sunday Thomas made three important decisions. One, he wanted to be a doctor, specifically an orthopedic surgeon. Two, his dad would always be his hero. And, three, although he didn't really like the scent of Old Spice, he would wear it every Sunday to honor his hero dad.

THOMAS REACHED HIS HOUSE WITHOUT INCIDENT. He put the sunflowers in a vase of water without taking the rubber band off. He thought about having a glass of chardonnay but decided he just wanted to take a shower and retire. He called Barbara after he was in his pajamas but didn't say anything about being followed or his spoiled surprise.

TWENTY-EIGHT

BARBARA AND ANITA WOKE SATURDAY TO A gloriously bright autumn day. The sky was cloudless and a soft-jazz blue; fall at the beach in California. Barbara had wondered how best to help her dear friend. She scanned through her memories of lessons learned and the countless books she had read. Since her retirement she had taken up the practice of yoga and meditation. She was confident she had ideas that might help but didn't know if Anita was ready to listen.

After a breakfast of oatmeal smothered in warm blue berries, melted butter with brown sugar and slivered almonds, the two ladies relaxed on the leather sofa looking out at the marriage of water and sky.

"Anita, how are you feeling today?" Barbara asked interrupting their quiet.

"Better, calmer. I'm not worried about my eye surgery. I know I'm in good hands. My arm is achy and heavy in this cast but not bad." She lifted up her casted arm to show Barbara.

"Well, I really didn't phrase my question accurately. I meant, mentally. How are you feeling mentally? Are you confident in your decision to leave Daryl?"

She nodded her head. "Yes, I am."

"What can I do to help you with this transition?" With both hands Barbara lifted a warm cup of green tea and took an unhurried sip.

"Well, first of all, I appreciate all that you are already doing. But, I might need a place to stay after the surgery during my recovery."

"Of course. You are welcome to stay at our house anytime."

As they sat on the sofa staring through the sliding glass door into the blue, Anita felt tiny tears trickle down her cheeks. She turned to Barbara and quietly said, "I think I've always had trouble with letting go of things."

"Letting what go?"

"Oh, I still have rumblings deep in my gut about my dad—about how he just left and basically abandoned us. It weighs on me, like an irksome hangnail that is always there."

Barbara grinned. "Letting go is an age old problem. We've all had to deal with it, but some of us are better at it." She rubbed the back of her neck.

"My mom once told me a Zen story that seemed to help me. I had Dad issues too."

Anita leaned over to the end table and took out a tissue, gently wiping her tears from her cheeks. "Tell it to me. Maybe it will help me too."

"Sure." Barbara uncrossed her legs and gently closed her eyes, allowing the total darkness to more keenly focus her memory. After a moment she fluttered her eyes open and said. "Here's how I remember it."

"Dear wise Barbara," Anita said, as she turned her body toward her friend. "I'm ready to listen and, hopefully, learn."

In an even, soft tone Barbara started, "The story is about two monks. One is old and one is much younger. They are traveling together on a long journey on foot. Due to the heavy rains there are deep puddles they have to cross. They reach a young woman dressed in her silken robes, looking very cross and impatient, standing near a large puddle. She is reprimanding her attendants whose hands are full of packages. The younger monk notices the woman. He says nothing and walks by, but the older monk picks her up. He carries her across the water and puts her down. She doesn't say anything or acknowledge him in any way."

Anita's tears had stopped flowing. Barbara took a deep breath and continued. "The two monks continue on their way in silence. After several hours of quiet the younger monk says, 'That woman back there was so selfish and rude but you picked her up and carried her. She didn't even say thank you.' The older monk slows his pace. He turns and replies, 'I set the woman down hours ago on the side of the puddle. Why are you still carrying her?'"

ANITA PUT HER ARM AROUND HER FRIEND ALLOWING herself to relax into the comfort of Barbara's sage story.

Barbara looked up at Anita who was gazing down at her bare feet.

"What are you thinking?" Barbara asked.

There was silence. Anita's face seemed to melt, softened by the gravity of the story and possibly tugged by some insight. She rubbed her casted arm in circular motions as if trying to sooth the pain. She stared out through the huge, clean glass window across the gleaming sky into an abyss. Thoughts swirled around Anita's brain as if a whirling wind had caught them and wouldn't let them go. Ideas were twirling, churning but not gripping. There was no peaceful landing place for her thoughts.

Barbara waited. Softly she murmured words she had often heard from one of her yoga teachers. "Be still and know that you are exactly where you are supposed to be."

She looked over at her friend. Delicate, tiny beads of tears seeped out the corners of Anita's eyes as the ancient Zen wisdom pricked through the tough shell of her wounded soul. She said, "I've held on to so many hurts for so long, letting them rule my decision-making process, letting them infect my judgment."

Barbara shifted closer to Anita on the couch, wrapping an arm around Anita's bent shoulders. "I'm here for you. Tell me what you are thinking."

Anita sighed. "It's time to let go of my anger at my biological father and the drunk driver who caused the accident that killed my mother. It's definitely time to let go of Daryl. He never loved me. And, I was at a place where I didn't love myself. I deserve more, much more. It's time to let go and take my life back."

Barbara held her friend tightly. Anita's shoulders straightened. She took a huge, deep breath and stood up from the couch and walked over to the window, staring out into possibilities.

"Today," she whispered. "Today, I'm letting go." She gestured with her arms dramatically throwing her invisible anger out the window. "I'm letting go and listening to my gut."

"Yes, you are."

TWENTY-NINE

B ARBARA AND ANITA LEFT THE SERENITY OF THE beach house to go back to the Kirkland home in Nesport so that Anita could have eye surgery which was scheduled for the following morning.

After they arrived Barbara busied herself in the kitchen making meatloaf, mashed potatoes and brown sugar carrots. Thomas and Anita settled into the caramel colored suede sofa in the family room. Anita was happy for the diversion, forcing her mind into medical mode; getting her off the roller coaster of emotions from the past days.

"How did it go while I was gone?" Anita asked.

"I did a comminuted distal femur repair Wednesday on one of your previous patients, Mrs. Ellen Downey. You had treated her for sciatica a couple years ago. She was in a car accident. The repair was relatively routine, no complications. She'll be fine."

Anita tried to listen, focus. Her shoulders eased as she pushed her own issues aside and thought about healing; fixing others instead of fixing herself.

How did I get here? What a mess I've made for myself. Now I've gotten Thomas and Barbara involved. I've been hiding, denying. I want ... I need to get back to my patients. Hopefully, it will be soon.

She was more than ready to get her eye surgery over with and her arm healed enough to return to her beloved occupation. *I wonder if I'm strong enough to face the future.*

After their hearty dinner of comfort food and lighthearted conversation including giggles from the ladies about their popcorn and chardonnay evenings at the beach, Anita excused herself, giving Thomas and Barbara some alone time. She changed into the flannel PJs Barbara had bought for her and slipped under the soft comforter. Weighted down by the cast, it was difficult to find a comfortable position to sleep.

Earlier, Thomas insisted she spend the night before her surgery with them reiterating that she was not imposing. Anita put up no objections. *I can relax in this house with my dear friends. I feel safe here. I trust them. I don't know what I'd do without them. Thank God they are here for me. I'm not ready to return to my house, even if Daryl isn't there. It's time for me to stand up for myself. I won't be another Nicole Simpson.*

Anita reprimanded herself. *Stop this talk about*

Nicole. Go to sleep. Tomorrow is a new day. You are on the road to recovery. You are supported by your friends. Finally, fitfully, she dozed off.

Barbara changed into her long cotton nightgown and vanilla fleece robe, padded down the hallway to see if Anita needed anything. She listened through the door and heard Anita's rhythmic breathing signaling sleep.

Barbara walked into her bedroom. Thomas was lying in their queen sized bed with his arm holding open the covers for Barbara. "Come here," he motioned. "We need to talk."

Barbara leaned over and gently kissed him on the lips. "I'll be right there."

She took off her robe and hung it on the hook in the bathroom, sat on the bed and slid off her slippers. The comforting familiarity enveloped her as she nestled under the covers next to her husband. He took her in his arms. She rested her head on his barrel chest and nudged close, her customary position after decades of marriage. Thomas nuzzled closer, pulling her gently to him, giving her a protective squeeze. She peered up at him.

"What is it?" she asked. "What's going on?" Thomas brushed a few short wayward strands of hair behind her ear. "Is there something you need to tell me? The flowers in the vase, that was unusual. I know you too well, Thomas. Something is bothering you."

"Yes, Barbara. There is." His mouth was suddenly dry, chalky. Words wove in and out of his brain searching for just the right ones. He wanted to tell her about being followed to the beach house but not alarm her; not scare her.

Her back stiffened. "What is it Thomas? What's going on?" She furrowed her brow.

He leaned down toward her. His breath slowed. He gently kissed her forehead. He cleared his throat. "I was on my way to see you late Friday afternoon." He paused. "I wanted to surprise you and Anita. That's why I bought the flowers."

Barbara sat up on her elbow. "You were? What happened?"

Thomas took a cleansing breath; exhaled slowly, deliberately collecting his thoughts. He arranged them in an order, like a dominos train, neatly spaced. He didn't want one thought to spill out too quickly and topple the entire train.

"I was followed."

"Followed? What do you mean you were followed?" Her cheeks tightened, her jaw froze.

Thomas sat up and turned on the light on his bedside table. Barbara sat up too.

"What's this all about?"

"I'm not sure, but before you get too excited, I called John Osborn as soon as I got home. He found out that the guy who was following me is a private investigator. He's an ex-police officer and John knows him well. He left him a message but John hasn't heard back from him yet."

"This isn't making much sense to me. How did

John find out the name of the guy following you?"

"I got his license plate number."

"You did? That was smart." Barbara reached for the back of her hair, nervously twisting it with her fingers. "Do you think Daryl is trying to find Anita?" She felt the room darken along with her thoughts. *This Daryl is more devious and dangerous than I thought. I know he's up to no good. Why would a private investigator be following Thomas?*

"Yes, I do think Daryl is trying to find Anita." Thomas gently reached for Barbara's hand bringing it down from the back of her head. "I'll take care of this. I have a plan but I want you to be extra careful. The two of you should go back to the beach house for Anita's recovery while John and I sort this out."

"But the guy followed you to the beach house? Why would we go back there?"

"No, he didn't get that far. I," he hesitated again. "I pulled off at this Italian Restaurant in Aptos. This is going to sound weird, but I sat down at a table with a man and woman and asked for their help."

"What?"

"I know. It sounds crazy and that's what I told this couple. It just so happened that the man that I sat with was Dr. Michael Johnson. He is a physician. It took some convincing but he and his wife believed me." Thomas hesitated. "It's a long story Barbara but I'm sort of tired now. I'd rather cuddle with you than relive Friday night. Can I tell you the rest in the morning?" He tried to hug her but she resisted.

"No. Don't leave me hanging like this. I'm wide awake now."

"Okay. Dr. Michael Johnson's wife, Lily, is a huge Colombo fan and she got all into what was happening when I told her about being followed. We saw the guy come into the restaurant. They knew the owner of Giovanni's and he helped me slip out the back door."

"Slip out the back door? That's sneaky. Clever too."

"Lily's the one who told me to get the guy's license plate number. Good thing I did. That's how John found out who was following me. I know it is wild to think about."

"At least you're home safely," she let out a big sigh. "This is a lot to process."

"You're telling me. Barbara, I'm going to take care of this. I wanted to tell you just so that you'll be extra careful."

"Are we safe at the beach?"

"Yes, you are. I believe it's safer than here. Daryl has been here. I'm sure Anita told him about our beach house but he's never been there. I wouldn't think he knows which house it is. Besides, the guards won't let him in. Please rest. I'll take care of everything."

He reached over and turned off the light. "Right now I want to hold my wife in my arms. I love you." He pulled her close to him and gently kissed her lips. His breathing slowed.

"I love you too. And, thanks for the flowers." Barbara rested her head on Thomas's chest.

He whispered, "There was wine too but we'll share it when things settle down."

"My dear, dear Thomas, what would I do if something happened to you?"

She nestled close to Thomas's familiar warm body. Her breathing slowly calmed and she fell into a peaceful sleep.

THIRTY

DARYL WASN'T GETTING ANY RESULTS FROM THE new private investigator he hired. He was more determined than ever to find his wife. He was actually thinking he might be able to talk her into reconciliation. He had done it before. He wasn't sure he wanted her back but he damn well wasn't going to let anyone else have her until he was done with her. *She's my wife, damn it. We married, until death do us part and for better or for worse. I'm going to find you, Bitch.* He suspected Anita might need surgery for either her arm or her eye or already had it. He came up with a scheme. He called Claire, the Operating Room Scheduler at Washington Hospital where Anita worked. He had had a little fling with her years ago and thought he could charm something out of her.

Claire was a petite brunette with round

chocolate-brown eyes. She picked up the phone with her manicured, polished nails, "Claire Williams, OR." She was dressed in light blue scrubs, tailored to her hour glass figure; her long hair twisted in a clip in the back of her head.

"Hi, Claire, its Daryl."

"Daryl?" her voice cracked as she recognized his familiar sexy voice. Goosebumps erupted on her arms.

"Hi sweetheart, it has been too long." He ran his fingers through his thick mane.

Daryl had dated Claire before he met Anita. Claire had just begun to fall in love with him when he dumped her. The break up was very hard on her, particularly since she had to see Anita in the Operating Room. Anita knew nothing of Claire but she knew that Anita was the one who stole her boyfriend away. She still had feelings for Daryl but had been forced to move on and was finally getting over him. Now, hearing Daryl's sultry voice, she couldn't help but conjure up memories of their intense relationship and passionate lovemaking. During their time together she remembered that Daryl had gotten aggressive when he drank but Claire could diffuse that with a romp in bed. He was a little rough with her but she liked that, a strong man.

His deep, husky voice brought tingles to her spine. "Claire, how about you meet me for a cocktail after your shift? We could meet at Taylor's, our old stomping ground."

Claire hesitated answering. She thought. *Do I really want to open up this can of worms?* She asked, "What is it Daryl? Why are you calling me?"

"Claire, I need a friend. Things aren't working out as I planned. We can talk about it over a drink, not on the phone. Please meet me at Taylor's and I'll tell you all about it." His voice was smooth, hard for Claire to resist.

Well, the least I can do is listen to what he has to say. She agreed to meet him at 5:30 p.m. although she got off two hours earlier. She was going to go home to shower and change out of her working scrubs and into something that would make him realize what he was missing.

THIRTY-ONE

Daryl, dressed in a tailored blue sport coat atop a starched white long sleeve shirt and pressed dark slacks, sat at a small round table toward the end of the dark bar nervously swirling the ice cubes in his scotch waiting for Claire. He was sure Claire would give him what he wanted. She had always been malleable, unlike that bitch, Anita, who had to be put in her place; toppled from her high horse.

He checked his Louis Vuitton watch for the third time in less than ten minutes. It was 5:38 p.m. and Claire had agreed to meet him at 5:30 p.m. She was late. He took a big swig of his drink then turned to the door just as Claire coolly sauntered over to him. She was wearing a bright ruby-red dress, scooped at the neckline and cinched at her tiny waist. It seductively hugged her rounded hips. He got a whiff of her vanilla and rosewood perfume. *I must ask her for the name of that perfume. It's so arousing.*

Daryl stood up, opened his arms and asked, "Do I get a hug?" She hesitated. "Come on," he insisted, "I really need a hug." He took Claire in his arms; former lovers with a history of intimacy. He pulled her into him and she softened into his body thinking, maybe he really misses me. She enjoyed the strength of his arms around her.

"Hi, handsome." She pulled away and sat down on the leather bar stool. Her long brown hair curled over her cheeks.

"Hi, Beautiful, have you missed me?" Daryl smiled.

"Sure I've missed you but this is quite a surprise. How are you? What's up?"

He touched her arm. "First, may I get you a glass of sauvignon blanc? Is it still your favorite?"

"Yes, you remembered." She smiled, her red lips slightly parted. She was still slightly fluttery; nervous and wondering why Daryl had called her.

After the wine was served Daryl scooted his bar stool closer to Claire. She sipped the cool flowery, peach wine and the two of them talked about Daryl's recent sales conference. Claire knew something was up since he had called her out of the blue. She hadn't heard from him in several months and it certainly wasn't just a coincidence that his wife was scheduled for eye surgery in the morning.

"How are things with Mrs. Doctor Anita?"

Daryl leaned in and whispered, "Things aren't working out the way I thought they would with Anita. You were right. I can't get you out of my mind."

"What? She isn't everything you thought she would be?" Claire sarcastically teased while batting her eyelashes. *Maybe he is thinking about leaving Anita, or is this just wishful thinking on my part? What does she have that I don't have … besides an M.D.?*

"What aren't you getting from her, Daryl?" She twisted her hair around her finger, putting slightly firmer pressure against his leg.

He didn't move, smiled and then said, "May I get you another glass of wine?"

The second glass of wine arrived, along with another scotch. Daryl softly stroked Claire's bare upper thigh; an intoxicating feeling for both of them. "Anita's got such a busy schedule and she's not paying attention to me," he complained. "You were right about her. She doesn't treat me like you did." Unconsciously, Claire's body responded; warming, tingling, aroused. *Daryl wants to rekindle our spark. He is thinking about leaving Anita.* She gazed, glassy eyed, at Daryl. "I didn't order this. I'm not going to be able to drive if I drink this. You'll have to take me home." Claire smiled seductively and took a sip.

"That shouldn't be a problem," he winked. He got close to her ear; his scotch breath on her cheek, and whispered. "I know Anita's scheduled for surgery soon, isn't she? When is it scheduled? What, exactly, is she having done? We had a fight and the bitch isn't talking to me. She had a nasty fall last week."

Claire turned and leaned in. Daryl got a peak of her pink lacey bra. Now, inches away from his lips she whispered, "You know I'm not supposed to tell you. I would be putting my neck on the line and I could lose my job."

He winked at her, "You're talking about me here. Seriously, Claire, why would I tell anyone? I wouldn't do anything to hurt you. Anita doesn't know about us."

Claire sighed. She wanted to believe him. She remembered their many trysts together and her body was now warm and damp, especially between her thighs. Her head was mushy but she still couldn't bring herself to tell. "Daryl, I can't."

Daryl took a deep breath and a gulp of scotch. He wondered if she could see his hard-on through his pants. He guided her hand on top of it.

"So, you have missed me? "

"Yes, I have. I have an idea. Here's what you can do." He leaned over her and grabbed a new bar napkin from the stack and removed a pen from his inside jacket pocket.

"Okay, I understand you can't tell me … but you can write something down on this napkin. No one will ever know."

Claire, her hands perspiring, her heart racing, her body throbbing with desire, took the pen from Daryl and wrote on the napkin. Then, she took the last big swig of wine and glided the napkin into Daryl's hand.

Daryl lifted up the napkin and looked at it. It said, *10:00 a.m. Monday.* He tore it in half and then in half again and again. He wadded it up into a ball and leaned over the bar signaling the bartender. "Buddy, can you throw this away for me?"

"Sure."

Lightheaded and wobbly, Claire stood and purred into Daryl's chest. "You're going to have to take me home now, Daryl."

"Of course, sweetie, I'll take you home."

"Is that all you're going to do?"

"I'll take you home all right, and I'll drive you home to ecstasy too, you, naughty, naughty girl. You deserve a spanking."

Tipsy, Claire stood. "Yes, I do and I know you're just the right man to give it to me."

Daryl wrapped his arm around her waist and they left the bar. When they got to Daryl's Porsche he opened the door like a gentleman, and she seductively sat down, her dress hiked up high over her creamy thighs. Daryl leaned across her, buckling her seatbelt. He kissed her passionately. She melted into him, parted her lips, and took his tongue.

"Drive me Daryl," she cooed. "Drive me home."

THIRTY-TWO

HONEY-LUST STILL OOZED FROM HER PORES AS she lay, her head sated in the crook of Daryl's neck. Claire softly listened to his whisper breath, inhaling and exhaling, as though a calm ocean tide was coaxing small children to sleep. The earth, having slowed its rotation during the last hour, leisurely regained momentum as her eyes fluttered open; the warm cocoon of her bed and Daryl's enveloped arms still earthy and moist on her body. Nothing, she thought, would ever melt her buttery bliss. Her thoughts, muted and round, came slightly into focus but she blanketed them down, closed her eyes and feather-drifted back to sleep.

Sometime during the wee morning hours Claire stirred and reached for Daryl. The weight of his muscular body was still imprinted on the mattress and his warmth still radiated onto the sheets but he wasn't there. In his place, in wide-spaced handwriting, he had left a note.

Darling – I didn't want to disturb Sleeping Beauty. I have an early morning East Coast sales call. I'll be in touch.

XO - D

Her muddled brain tried to focus on his written words, and her thoughts brought her back to their sweltering night. She wondered if their lovemaking was a sign that he was finally considering leaving Anita and getting back together with her. He really should divorce her, she thought. *That was luxurious last night.* She inhaled his musty scent but her thoughts kept ricocheting back and forth ... he loves me, he loves me not.

I knew he'd be back. Something is definitely not right between those two.

He really cares about me.

Why did he need to find out from me when her surgery is scheduled?

Maybe he still loves me.

Does he want me or is he just using me?

Closing her eyes, disintegrating the euphoria of the night, her mood sharply shifted. She remembered the one time he really scared her. She thought he might even punch her. It was over something so vague she couldn't even remember why he had gotten so irate but she remembered the aftermath.

It was at the San Francisco Hyatt. He and Claire had gone to dinner with a close friend of his and were having a delightful time over after-dinner drinks when, out of nowhere, he made a curt comment to Claire, slammed his drink on the table and told his friend that he and Claire were leaving. As soon as the two of them got into the elevator and the doors closed he yanked her toward him, his sickly-sweet liquor-breath steamed out in his words. "If you ever embarrass me again in front of my friends it will be the last time." Then, he shoved her back against the hard elevator wall and turned his back on her. When the elevator door opened, he stomped down the hall and into their room without saying another word to her all night. She slept fitfully, half-awake with one eye open, replaying over and over what had happened and what could have possibly set him off. Thoughts crept into her consciousness, jagged, rusty mind. *Would he have hurt me? Could he?*

She remembered that Daryl acted a little off when they met last night, not his usual salesman upbeat, buoyant persona.

Claire had tucked the elevator incident in a locked suitcase in her mind. She never brought it up to him and had convinced herself that she had caused the problem. Claire was an expert at diffusing his temper, knowing the subtle hints in his demeanor, the hiccups in his rationale, and she would calmly change the situation without his realization. After all, she had been programmed her entire childhood to walk on pin and needles, and dodge poison-laden arrows so as not to unleash her father's drunken rages.

DARYL DIDN'T HAVE AN EARLY MORNING MEETING. Instead he headed to Alamo Car Rental. He knew he couldn't drive his Porsche around while looking for Anita. He rented a white Toyota Camry and headed to the hospital. He parked close to the main entrance where he knew Anita would be entering and exiting. He didn't get there in time to see Anita heading into the entrance but he knew she was there. He sat in his car with a thermos of coffee and a banana nut muffin and waited and waited, eyes transfixed to the door.

THIRTY-THREE

L YING PRONE ON THE GURNEY, HER RIGHT EYE
bandaged in gauze, Anita was wheeled into the
recovery room. The golden yellow on the top part of
her cheek faded into the white gauze.

Dr. Andy Chen, clad in blue hospital-issue
surgery scrubs, walked out of the operating room
with Dr. Thomas Kirkland following closely behind.
Thomas wrapped his burly arm around Andy's
shoulder. "You did a fine job. Surgery was successful.
Her right eye entrapment is relieved and should heal
with no side effects. Anita should be back to her old
self with no double vision."

With straightened posture, Andy acknowledged
the compliment, "Thanks, Thomas."

"It was a pleasure to assist you and watch your
expertise and delicate manipulations of her eye socket.

You've got all my referrals for any facial fractures in the future. I sure hope I don't see a lot of them but if I do, you're the man."

The two doctors walked into the surgery waiting room where Barbara sat staring at a well-worn magazine. She stood up when they entered. Andy spoke. "Everything went well, just as expected. She's in recovery and will be ready for company in a short while. She'll be ready to leave in a couple hours. Thomas said you were thinking of going to the beach house, but I'd like her to stay in town for at least a day. I don't anticipate any problems but for the first 24 hours, as with all my patients, I would like her in town."

"Okay." Barbara shook Dr. Chen's hand. He left the waiting room. Thomas stood beside Barbara and signaled toward some empty chairs in the corner of the room. "Let's sit down over here."

The two of them took their seats. Thomas leaned close to his wife. "I was very impressed with Dr. Chen. That's the good news." Barbara looked puzzled. He hesitated, "I know Anita will recover well but, um, I didn't get a chance to tell you all the details about being followed."

"There's more?"

"I'm a bit more concerned after talking with John Osborn this morning. John found out the name of the owner. It belongs to a guy named Benjamin Carrey. John knows him very well. Carrey is an ex-police officer and now a private eye. John had used him on a couple cases."

"Gosh, this is getting so complicated. It's making me very nervous."

"We'll all be okay." Thomas patted Barbara's knee. "I have a plan. Since you can't go back to the beach house tonight per Andy's instructions and you can't—"

"What is going on Thomas? You have to tell me."

"Daryl's been at our house looking for Anita."

Barbara glared at him; a razor-sharp stare. "You didn't tell me Daryl had been to our house. This guy is creepy. What do we do?"

"I've booked two adjoining rooms at the Best Western tonight. I'll join you after my evening rounds. I'll pick up some Chinese food for dinner. We'll eat out of little white boxes like we use to do when we were dating."

"What will I tell Anita?" She turned her gaze toward the wall then down to the industrial blue carpet.

Thomas stood up. "I've asked the recovery nurse to let me know when Anita is ready for visitors. I'm going to go change and see a patient. I'll meet you in recovery soon."

THE NURSE CAME INTO THE WAITING ROOM AND got Barbara. "I've already called Dr. Kirkland to let him know Anita is fully awake."

Barbara walked up to Anita's bed, leaned toward her, smelling the antiseptic on her face, and whispered, "Hi, Anita. It went well."

Slowly blinking her non-bandaged eye, Anita said, "That's good. I am so ready to have this all behind me."

"Would you like some ice chips or a cracker?"

"Ice chips would be nice." She sounded like she was chewing cotton. "It's beach time soon. I'm nearly ready for my bathing suit."

BARBARA SAW THOMAS WALKING TOWARD HER AS she returned with the ice chips and the two of them walked into Anita's curtained recovery room. Thomas leaned over toward Anita and tenderly kissed her crown. "Andy did a fine job. How are you feeling?"

"Sleepy."

"That's good. It's good to get your rest, but I wanted to let you know it all went so well. I've got to see some patients but I'll see you for dinner though."

Barbara looked at Thomas. "Thomas, let's talk to Anita about our evening plans."

"Yes, we'll all be spending tonight at the beautiful Best Western in town before the two of you head to the beach house tomorrow. Dr. Chen wants all his patients to stay in town for the first twenty-four hours post-operatively."

"I thought we were going to your house."

Thomas said, "Daryl's been there. He's looking for you. I think it's best if we stay away from the

234

house tonight. You and Barbara can head to the beach tomorrow."

ANITA'S THOUGHTS WERE FUZZY AND DULL. WORDS hovered over her like floating ghosts but none came out. Anita nodded. Barbara helped Anita sit up and take a few ice chips.

"How does Chinese food at the Best Western sound to you? I called the hotel and made reservations for adjoining rooms so you don't have to worry about that." He kissed Barbara's cheek, patted Anita's arm, and left.

Barbara was a little anxious. She still had a lot more questions about Daryl coming to the house, but she knew that Thomas would fill her in soon. Hopefully it would be tonight at the hotel when Anita was sleeping.

ANITA WAS RELEASED FROM THE HOSPITAL AND THE women drove directly to the Best Western where Anita waited in the car as Barbara checked in. Once in their rooms Barbara gave Anita a Percocet and tucked her into bed. "I'll be right next door. I'll leave the adjoining door ajar so you can call me if you need anything. I left water and some leftover recovery crackers on the nightstand—yummy, dry saltines. Call me if you need anything. Get some rest." Barbara leaned into Anita, kissing the top of her matted hair and tiptoed into her adjoining room leaving the door slightly ajar.

IN HER DRUG INDUCED SLEEP ANITA HEARD A rapping on the door. As the knocking got louder Anita rolled over in bed thinking she must be dreaming. Then, there was a louder knock. She focused her eye on the nightstand clock. It was 4:30 p.m. Thomas wasn't expected until after six. It's got to be Barbara, she thought. *She must have forgotten her key.* Slowly, groggily she stumbled to the door and unlatched the top chain. As she was reaching the door to turn the door knob, Barbara came around and grabbed her hand.

"What are you doing?" Barbara hissed.

Shocked, Anita turned her head around. Thoughts bombarded the inside of her skull, jumbled. They seemed to run together, on and on, bouncing off one another. "I thought, wait, I thought you locked … you locked … wait … you locked yourself out." She shook her head. "Who's knocking?" Anita focused her eye on Barbara, dumbfounded.

Barbara tugged Anita's left hand away from the door. "I don't know, Anita, but you're not opening that door. No one is supposed to know we're here." Barbara steered Anita through the adjoining door, slamming it closed and locking it.

"I thought it was you. I thought you forgot your key."

Barbara picked up the phone and dialed the front desk.

THIRTY-FOUR

ANITA WOBBLED BACK AND FORTH ON THE BED trying to find her grounded center. With her ear to the phone Barbara said, "Anita, are you okay? What? What are you talking about? I didn't forget my key. I'm right here, Anita. I've been in the adjoining room. Please just sit on the bed. I'm calling security." Anita slumped to her side and lay down.

With shaking hands and voice, Barbara spoke. "There is someone knocking on our door. We are not expecting company. Please come and check it out."

The perky front desk clerk explained away the situation, "Someone must have gotten rooms mixed up. Don't be worried. I'll have security check it out for you. Is there anything else I can do?"

"No, just come by as soon as possible and check

out who is knocking on our door." Barbara hung up the phone and sat on the bed next to Anita. Her mind was racing.

OUTSIDE THE DOOR, DARYL FROWNED AND GREW impatient as no one answered. He rejected the idea of knocking louder because he didn't want to create a scene. Instead, he trudged away from Anita's room and got back into his rented Toyota. *I'll have to come up with a better plan. This isn't working. She's not answering the door. Damn Bitch.*

SECURITY CAME TOO LATE. NO ONE WAS THERE.

That evening, Thomas brought Chinese food to their hotel rooms for dinner. Barbara and Anita told Thomas what had happened and that Security found no one at the door. Thomas wasn't convinced they were safe. He was glad that he was spending the night and, as an added precaution, he asked Anita to switch rooms with him and Barbara. After finishing their Won-ton soup and broccoli beef, the ladies switched rooms.

During the night everything was quiet in the room, but Thomas slept fitfully wondering how best to protect Anita and Barbara.

The next morning, Thomas rose early and showered to go to the hospital. Barbara was happy that he had stayed and had convinced herself that the knocking was probably just someone who had gotten the rooms mixed up, as the hotel clerk suggested. Thomas still was not so sure. He had left the adjoining door open during the night. He warned the ladies not to open the main doors for anyone. He also asked Security to be vigilant about not allowing anyone access to their rooms.

Barbara was still in bed, awake and resting when Thomas got up, showered and shaved for the day. He went to the lobby to get her some coffee and returned to the room.

He handed the coffee to Barbara. "Thank you, Thomas." Barbara sat up and brushed a kiss on Thomas's cheek.

"Be safe. I love you. Call me before you two head for the beach house this afternoon. Call the front desk to have someone escort you to your car."

"I will. We'll be fine. Thanks for dinner and a sleepover last night. I love you too." Barbara's lips turned into a grin, honoring her man, her protector.

When Thomas left the room, Barbara got out of bed and put the chain on the door. She got back in bed, sat up and pulled the comforter up to her chin. She sipped her warm, cream-filled coffee allowing the caffeine to awaken her foggy brain. She was looking forward to the beach later today; to her own bed at the beach house, the endless sky, the sand in her toes, and some peace and quiet. Because of the guard and a gate into their housing development, no unexpected guests would be knocking at her beach house door.

After she finished her coffee, she got up, tiptoed to the open connecting door. Anita was snug under the covers. She listened as slow, rhythmic breaths announced sleep. Barbara went into her bathroom to take a quick shower.

THOMAS GOT TO THE PARKING LOT AND INTO HIS car. *I don't feel comfortable with this situation. I know Daryl has been looking for Anita. I need to get some help, make sure my ladies are safe.*

Daryl slouched down in the Toyota two cars away watching Thomas leave.

THIRTY-FIVE

THOMAS SLOWLY PULLED OUT OF THE HOTEL parking lot anxious to get to the office. *I'm going to call John Osborn and ask for some help. He'll have some ideas. This has gotten way out of hand. Maybe I should hire a bodyguard for Barbara and Anita.*

DARYL STAYED TUCKED DOWN IN HIS RENTAL CAR. His right eye twitched as he heard the rumbling diesel engine of Thomas's Mercedes pulling out of the lot. When the noise was barely audible, he inched up and anxiously peeked, checking his surroundings. The parking lot was quiet. *Should I try again?* His heart was thudding, fueled by adrenalin, dancing in his chest, but he wasn't interested in getting caught. He sat thinking. *You could get her now. Thomas is gone.* He let out an audible sigh. *Then again, maybe it's just not the right time. Something isn't right.*

Instead of going back into the hotel, he decided that he had had enough for the last two days. He needed to get into his office to make an appearance. He had already missed some important sales calls. He didn't want anyone talking about his absences. He stared blankly at the drab beige outside walls of the hotel and snarled under his sour coffee breath. "Anita, there will be another time. I'm not done with you, Bitch."

He put the Camry in reverse and backed out of the parking space. "I'm tired of driving this piece of shit rental car. Give me back my wings."

He arrived at the rental car agency, flung the keys at the attendant and said, "I'm in a hurry. I'm done with this car. Here's your Camry. Keep the charges on my Visa."

He trudged the three blocks to the mechanics shop where had had left the Porsche. When he got in his car he breathed in the rich scent of leather, wrapped his strong hands around the gear shift, and sped to his office. *I'm not done with you yet, Cunt.*

THIRTY-SIX

ANITA AND BARBARA MADE IT FROM THE BEST Western to the beach house without incident.

It had been a relaxing few days so far and Anita's recovery was going well. Her eyesight was normal; the bruising almost gone. She felt stronger. Her right arm was no longer painful yet still cumbersome in the cast. She and Barbara had many long walks and deep conversations interspersed with calm and quiet. The two had a rhythm, an understanding, like an old married couple. They knew when to probe, be silent, or joke and laugh. Anita absorbed Barbara's strength and compassion. She reminded Anita of her mother. Like Louise, Barbara could be quiet and contemplative for long periods of time. Each day Barbara led Anita through guided meditation. It helped Anita sleep and find a sense of calm in the whirlwind.

With their hands wrapped around delicate china cups filled with freshly steeped warm chamomile tea, the two women sat in silence on the plush leather sofa looking out at the endless muted blue sky. Barbara picked up a book from her coffee table. It was Robin Heerens Lysne's, *Living a Sacred Life*. Barbara read from it often for inspiration. She turned to page 183 and read aloud. "October 27, Solitude. Today I listen to my heart garden and rest in the peace I find there."

"What a coincidence," Anita said. "I was just thinking about quiet and Mom. Now you read this passage. We truly are in-synch." She continued, "I remember asking Mom about her stillness and quiet. She was very good at it. She told me that when she was quiet, she could hear her heart sing. She said it was the most beautiful of songs." Anita took a sip of her tea. She finally thought she understood what her mom and, now, Barbara was talking about when they mentioned quiet, still, solitude. She said, "I think I'm beginning to hear my heart sing."

"Wow, that's beautiful."

Out the glass door, a squadron of pelicans smoothly swooped down, closer to the water.

"Shall I read another passage?"

"Sure."

"October 28, Melancholy. Today I give myself permission to go within and feel what I feel."

"Wow. That hits home. I think this book could be quite useful for me."

Barbara handed the book to Anita. "Here, take mine. I'll get another copy."

The two women used this book during their tea time as a catalyst for many deep conversations before Barbara's afternoon naps.

"REMEMBER THE ZEN STORY I TOLD YOU LAST TIME we were here?"

"Yes."

"My mom use to tell me all these stories when I was young. It's funny. I didn't really get them until I was much older. She told me this one when I was dating a guy in college that she didn't like. She thought he was too controlling. Here's the story."

In her calm voice she said, "A horse came galloping quickly down the road with a man on its back. It seemed as though the man had someplace very important to go. Another man who was standing alongside the road shouted, 'Where are you going in such a hurry?' The man on the horse shouted as he sped by, 'I don't know. Ask the horse.'"

Anita smiled and said, "Are you trying to say I've been letting Daryl lead me in the wrong direction?"

"As my mom used to say, 'it's a story for you to interpret.'"

"So, how did you interpret the story?"

Barbara said, "Me? My mom was right about the boy I was dating. I was blindly following him down a dark path. I needed to get off that horse. It took more than my mom's story to set me straight but eventually, I got out of that relationship."

Anita nodded. "Um ... I use to always be the one guiding the horse, but I let go of the reins with Daryl."

Barbara raised her eyebrows. "Maybe. Maybe it's time to take them back. Is your brain too full of Zen lessons, or are you interested in one more story I've just remembered?"

"I'm interested, but first more tea or would you prefer wine?" she asked. Anita got up from the couch. She walked into the kitchen, got the wine bottle out of the refrigerator, brought it to the table and poured herself a glass. She sat down and rolled her shoulders back. She placed her cast on the armrest. "I'm ready to listen."

Barbara began, "Okay. There is a pair of acrobats. A teacher and her student, a young girl. They perform each day on the streets to earn money for food. The performance consists of the teacher balancing a pole on her head while the petite girl climbs up to the top of the pole. She remains there while the teacher walks around. They each have to maintain complete focus and balance to prevent an accident.

"One day the teacher says to the young girl, 'How about I watch you and you watch me, so that we can help each other maintain our concentration and balance? That way we can help prevent an accident.'

246

"The young girl replied, 'Dear Master. I believe it would be better if we each watched our self. To look after one self means we are looking after both of us.'"

Anita said, "That certainly was an astute child."

"Yes, I believe so." Barbara continued, "How would you interpret this story?"

Anita said, "This one is pretty straight forward. I think it means by taking care of yourself you are ultimately taking care of others. In fact, if you don't take care of yourself you won't be able to take care of others." Anita looked into Barbara's eyes. "Your mom was a very clever woman and so are you, my dear friend. Thank you for sharing these stories with me."

Barbara got up from the couch. "Thank you for listening. I hope they will help. I'm going to retire now. My brain is very full." She walked around the couch. Anita stood and the two women hugged.

"Thank you, mine too."

Barbara padded toward her bedroom. Anita lay down, cocooned in private thought.

ON THEIR LAST DAY AT THE BEACH ANITA WALKED on the sand alone. She stopped and turned around admiring her solo foot prints. The droopy brim of her large, white cotton hat covered her forehead. It gently flopped in the breeze as her bare feet skimmed across the soft, cool sand. She listened to the calming of rolling waves as the seagulls squawked their hunger song. The fog, distant in the horizon, left a dewy, salty mist that moistened her skin. *It's been a relaxing time at the beach filled with healing and laughter, and I know I can do what I need to do.* Although Anita's hand injury still prevented her from performing surgery, she was ready to return to the real world and her much loved orthopedic practice.

Anita drew in a huge breath of crisp, salty air and looked out over the water, sitting back down on the sand. She stared into the blue abyss of sea and sky. Tiny tears welled in the corners of her eyes then trickled down her cheeks. She scooped handfuls of warm sand, lifting them to eye level then slowly pouring the tiny granules back to earth, imaging the sand to be her worries and the earth the solutions. She wished she had made better choices. She wasn't completely ready to accept all the reasons she got involved with Daryl and married him, but she was definitely feeling like she could better align her choices with her values.

Anita recalled Barbara's wise words last night. "The beach teaches you about life. Listen to what it is trying to say. Just as the ocean and the beach never look the same, altered by the changing of the tides, the wind and waves, creatures in the sea and on land, by shells, driftwood and footprints, so will be your problems. Although this all seems monumental today, tomorrow will bring a new perspective."

Anita continued the methodic action of dipping her hands in the sand, scooping up handfuls, letting them trickle between her fingers alternating with dropping the sand in one swift pour. As she dug deeper the sand cooled to her touch. It was malleable. It grew wet and clumpy forming a ball-shape as she dropped the scoop.

Her mind scrambled with thoughts but the self-deprecation, eased. She closed her eyes and listened. *Was she really hearing the stiff-legged prance of the sandpipers playing wave-tag? Could she hear the wind whisper, the pelicans squawk as they soared in military-like fashion above her? What was nature telling her?*

The sandpipers never tumbled in the waves. The wind calmed but never stopped. The pelicans got out of formation but could re-group with new members seamlessly. *Lessons? Are these some of the lessons Barbara spoke of?*

She quietly whispered, "Mom, I miss you so much. I know you're here beside me. I'm stronger now. I feel you in the wind. I hear you in Barbara's voice—my surrogate mother." She bent her head down toward the sand and closed her moist eyes. "I love you, Mom. It's going to be okay. Thank you for all the life lessons. I can feel your resilience. You believed in me—told me to never give up. I'm not going to. I'm sorry I didn't always listen but I'm better and stronger now. I will make you proud. I'm determined to start my life anew." Anita picked up her journal and wrote.

Mom, I Carry You with Me
Enveloped in my heart
Like soft boiled eggs
Warm, foamy milk
Childhood memories
Fresh sweet Snickerdoodles
Floating pink spring blossoms
I can't bring you back
But I hear your whisper breath on my shoulder
Like cooing, morning Meadowlark
Transforming grief on drifting clouds
Into self-compassion, forgiveness

Words, fueled by her mother's love, channeled through her fingers and onto the pages of her journal. She wrote another poem.

It's Time
Seashells crunch under my feet
Frayed memories
Meshing with grains of sand
Burying my soles

Faint outlines
Of my recent past
Float slowly through clouds
Mayhem and flashbacks
Heavy cast, reminder on arm

Wind broadcasts time
A marriage, begging to forget
Erase scars and broken bones
Frazzled life, draws a line

Before and after
Churning waves filter heavy from light
Clouds cushion as wind scatters
Raw emotions filter fear, anger, and shame

I rise to new beginnings, determined to absolve
Loneliness, hurt, bitterness
Embrace courage, self-respect, truth
My fresh resolve

THIRTY-SEVEN

BARBARA GAZED OUT THE FLOOR-TO-CEILING living room window staring at Anita and thought, she's been through a lot, poor thing. *It's nice to see her almost back to her old self.* She turned around and went into the master bedroom to finish packing.

ANITA SAT QUIETLY ON THE BEACH, HER JOURNAL IN her lap, her feet buried in the sand along with her thoughts. A handful of people walked along the edge of the water on a semi-private beach. The owners of the homes had access to the long stretch of pristine beach. There was a public entrance about two miles away but rarely did people wander this far down from that access. Anita opened her fluttery, day-dreaming eyes and noticed a striking-looking man dressed in blue shorts and a pale yellow, collared shirt walking toward her. *He's definitely not from around here with that attire. At least, I've never seen him here before.* She shyly smiled as he got near.

"Hello," he said in a thick German accent, "Are you from around here? My name is Karl."

His square jaw had a couple days golden growth of beard; his eyes cobalt blue. His muscular arms tugged at his shirt sleeve, his body bronzed from the sun.

"Hi. I'm Anita Stone. "I don't live here but I come here often and know the area well."

"I was wondering if you could recommend a nice place nearby for dinner—nothing too fancy as we'll be taking our two-year-old, Emma, with us." His deep voice was throaty; his words crisp. "My wife and I are on holiday from Munich. We've been in the U.S. for four weeks and will be returning home in two days. I'd like to treat them to a nice dinner before we return to Germany."

Anita felt flushed. Her stomach flip-flopped, like a fish on a hook. The hairs on the back of her neck stood upright. She didn't know exactly why.

Oh, yes you do. You know exactly why you're uncomfortable so close to a man. My reaction is an automatic impulse now after all those months with Daryl making accusations of me seeing other men. If Daryl were here he'd ... don't know what he'd do, but he'd definitely accuse me of something. My body is now programmed to that jerk. You're doing nothing wrong Anita, just speaking to a man.

Anita took a second breath and relaxed before speaking. "Have you enjoyed your time here, Karl?"

"Very much so. This is our last stop. Here, in California, we've been from San Francisco to Los Angeles. It's so warm here. We are already getting drifts of snow at home. We've been driving a lot and Petra, my wife, recently learned that we are expecting another baby. She's been very tired. I'm glad we rented this house from my old college roommate for our last week before we return home to Germany. Emma loves the sand. Petra and Emma are napping now."

"How lovely. Congratulations." Anita turned her head slightly and pursed her lips together, trying to think of a nice restaurant nearby. She didn't notice a man sitting on the wooden stairs next to Barbara's house but ... Daryl had seen enough. He bolted upright. "Damn Bitch. I knew she was cheating on me. Now I have proof."

He stomped to the back door of the Kirkland house and yanked open the sliding glass door and tromped in. Barbara heard the slider and called, "Are you back already? I'm not finished packing yet."

Daryl stomped into the master bedroom; his gun in his jacket pocket, his hand wrapped around the grip.

Startled, Barbara dropped the folded clothes in her hands and froze. "Daryl," her words came out squeaky, "What are you doing here?"

Starkly, he answered, "What do you think I'm

doing? I'm here to see my wife, the cheating bitch."

BARBARA'S PALMS PERSPIRED. "CALM DOWN DARYL. What are you talking about?" Barbara's mind raced thinking back to her years of training on handling volatile situations.

All those training seminars as a school administrator and principal, and I never had to use them until now. Remember, remember. Call 911. Listen to emotion without showing emotion. Speak softly. Move slowly. Be calm. Get to a safe place.

She took a deep breath. "Daryl, Anita and I are here relaxing as she recovers from her eye surgery. Let's go into the living room and talk." She moved a couple steps toward the bedroom door where she would have a clear view of Anita. "I'm sure we can settle this." She took a slow, deep breath and relaxed her shoulders.

DARYL WAS FIDGETY. HIS RIGHT HAND WAS IN HIS pocket. "I saw her on the beach talking to her lover."

"What? What are you talking about, Daryl? There must be some misunderstanding."

"Right. You can't fool me. I just saw her on the beach talking with her lover." Daryl's body stiffened angrily and he shifted back and forth on his heavy feet.

"Daryl, please, let's go into the living room and sit down."

"I've already seen enough." His sweating palm moistened the grip of the gun.

Daryl moved close to Barbara. His breath reeked of alcohol. He pulled the gun out of his pocket, his hand shaking. Large goosebumps rose on Barbara's arms as she saw the pistol. *He's drunk and has a gun. He's serious. He might kill us. God, help us.*

"You and I have nothing to discuss. This is between me and my cheating bitch of a wife."

"Daryl, please, you don't want to do this." She tried to take a deep breath but her lungs were filled with wet concrete. She forced air down into tiny open tubes in her lungs.

"Sure I do. Yeah, let's go into the living room. I'll show you my wife's lover. He's on the beach with her right now." He pushed the gun into Barbara's side. "Let's go."

"I'm going, Daryl. You don't need to be rough with me." Barbara's back stiffened and her shoulders tensed up her neck. Her breath was thin, her legs wobbly, the floor uneven as if there was an earthquake.

She looked through the windows. Anita was sitting on her beach towel alone.

THIRTY-EIGHT

DARYL STARED THROUGH THE SLIDING GLASS
door. Anita was by herself. *Where is he hiding? I
just saw them together.* He snarled his upper lip and
looked at Barbara. "The two of you are trying to hide
something from me, aren't you?"

"No," Barbara said as calmly as she could.
"Daryl, let's sit down. No one is hiding anything from
you."

Abruptly, the teakettle whistled. Both Daryl and
Barbara jerked. "It's the tea kettle. I was making a cup
of tea." Barbara started toward the kitchen, Daryl in
lockstep behind her.

"Turn that damn thing off," he roared.

"I'm going to. That's where I'm headed."

Her nerves were on edge, her stomach
somersaulted, and the teakettle shrilly whistled, but

surprisingly Barbara's voice came out as smooth as warm milk, just like she had been trained to do. "I'm turning the kettle off." She turned toward it and took it off the stove. The incessant shriek fizzled out.

What should I do now? I have this boiling water I could use, throw it on his face or his hand but that's really no match for a drunk with a gun. That would be foolish, Barbara. Stay calm. Think. Tuck your shoulders in your back pocket, remember?

Daryl jerked the gun around, "Hurry up."

"Daryl, there's got to be some sort of mix-up. We can settle this, but it's not the time or place. You shouldn't be here."

"But I am here and I'm going to talk to *my wife.*"

They were still standing in the kitchen. Daryl's sickly sweet alcohol stench secreted from his pores. *What can I do? Maybe I should try to feed him. It will sober him up a bit, bide me some time.*

"Daryl, you must be hungry. We have some leftover pizza in the fridge. Let me heat it up for you," she stuttered. "Or, I could make you some scrambled eggs and toast." She placed her wobbly hand on the refrigerator door handle.

"I'm not hungry," he said through a grimaced face. "I'm here to see Anita. Let's go back into the living room. Hurry up." His voice was loud and nasty.

He's drunk and could shoot me, not even meaning to. She spoke slowly, "Daryl, put the gun down. We're peaceful people. You're a peaceful man. There's no need for a gun."

Growing impatient, Daryl wagged the gun at Barbara and took a few steps toward the living room where he had a better view of Anita. "Get over here," he ordered. "I'm watching you."

"I'm coming, Daryl." *Address him by his name. Make the conversation personal. Think, Barbara, think of all your training. Oh my god. He's getting angrier and angrier.*

Daryl's gaze ping-ponged from Anita at the water's edge to Barbara in the kitchen. When he was looking through the windows toward Anita, Barbara flipped the handset off the desk-top telephone under the pass-through, hidden from Daryl. She punched in 911 and faked a coughing spell so that Daryl would not hear the operator.

"Nine one one. What is your emergency?" Barbara coughed again but didn't speak. She hurried back into the living room.

The 911 operator listened to the muddled voices. The address where the call originated displayed on her computer screen.

"You shouldn't be here. You know there's a restraining order on you."

The operator remained silent.

"You don't know anything about Anita and me, Barbara. This is between a husband and his wife."

"Daryl, why do you have a gun? You don't need a gun." She enunciated the word 'gun' slowly and clearly.

That's all the 911 operator needed to hear. She dispatched an officer to the Kirkland beach house.

THIRTY-NINE

ANITA WALKED UP THE WOODEN STEPS breathing in the salty, moist clean air. She stopped at the top step and sat down to put on her rubber flip flops. She looked up as diamonds sparkled on the water's surface. The whole world seemed a little brighter. *It's going to be okay. I've got this.* Her posture straightened. *My new resolve is to get back my life.* "Mom, you would be proud of me again," she whispered in the breeze. She got up and walked to the back of the beach house on the secluded stone pathway. She was temporarily out of sight.

Barbara's spoke loudly hoping Anita could hear her. "Daryl, put the gun away. You don't need it. I'm sure we can come to some sort of understanding. We're peaceful people here, you and I." *I hope the 911 operator is sending help.* There was no noise coming from the phone in the kitchen.

Barbara heard the outdoor water turn on, knowing that Anita was washing off her feet. *Stay outside longer, Anita. Don't come in. Don't come up the steps to the back deck.*

Roughly, Daryl pushed Barbara away from the windows toward the corner of the room. Barbara heard the water go off and waited.

"Stop Anita, don't come in here." Her voice quaked out from her dry lips.

Daryl slammed the pistol against Barbara's face. Instantly, her lip split. Crimson blood pooled in the corner of her mouth. He pointed the gun at her, "Shut up. Don't even think about saying another word." He smacked her down on the carpet. Blood ran down the side of her split lip and dripped ruby red on the plush cream colored carpet as she fell.

She looked up at Daryl. "Daryl, stop. This isn't necessary."

Anita sat down on the wooden bench and toweled off her feet. She didn't hear the commotion inside the house.

"You, shut up. Stand up and get over here." His voice mean and in a forced husky whisper. He stood sternly in the corner of the room.

Barbara's thoughts raced. *I need to bide time. Where are the police? Are they coming? They have to be.* "I am getting up but it takes me a little while. I don't move like I used to, you know. There's no need to push me. I'm not going to fight you." *How do I keep him occupied?*

Please, Anita, don't come in here.

She finally stood, jelly for legs, and got to the corner. She saw Anita standing on the deck at the sliding door. Daryl alternately pointed the gun at Barbara and then at the slider.

Standing on the deck Anita noticed the door was ajar. *That's not like Barbara to leave the door open.* That's weird, she thought. And, even though her stomach momentarily tightened, she dismissed her concern.

As she walked into the house, she called out, "Barbara?" She turned to close the slider and heard Daryl's low growling-like voice, "Surprise Anita."

Startled, Anita's body wrenched around. She saw Barbara with her swollen, bloody lip and her rumpled, blood-stained blouse. Barbara was trembling in front of Daryl.

Anita's jaw twitched. In a raspy voice, she said, "What are you doing here Daryl? What's going on? Why …?" She saw the gun aimed at Barbara's back and froze. She licked her dry lips. Her jaw tightened. She wanted to run. Her mind flashed. *He has a gun. I can't run. I can't put Barbara in more danger. What am I going to do? How did he find me? Oh, my god. This is awful.*

"I saw you on the beach with your lover, you cheating bitch."

Anita was confused. "Daryl, what are you talking about?" She felt perspiration well in her arm pits.

"Don't give me that. I saw you. You're cheating on me. I knew it all along." Daryl's slurred words were evil sounding.

"No, I'm not cheating. I was just sitting on the beach. There's no lover." She shook her head.

Daryl leaned out from behind Barbara, still pointing the gun at her back.

"Don't hurt Barbara," Anita pleaded, her voice shaky. "She has done nothing to you."

Faintly, Barbara heard police sirens in the distance. *Hurry ... hurry.*

"I didn't come here to hurt Barbara, but you've put her in this situation by bringing your lover to her house. This is entirely your fault, you lying bitch."

"Daryl, there's no lover. I don't know what you're talking about."

"Shut up, whore. I saw him out there with you." The veins in Daryl's temples swelled blue.

"No. There isn't anyone." Anita's casted arm trembled. "Daryl, are you talking about the man on the beach a few minutes ago? That was a guy from Germany asking for a restaurant recommendation for dinner tonight for him and his family. I talked to him about two minutes. Daryl, please let Barbara go," Anita pleaded. "This has nothing to do with her. Let her go." She flashed back to all Daryl's other accusations about men; imagined lovers. She could never convince him there was no one else. She stepped cautiously toward Daryl.

Barbara slowly turned to face Daryl. His alcohol stench stung her being. "Daryl, let's work this out peacefully. You don't want to do anything rash."

"I'm here to talk to my wife and you're my ticket

to her. Come over here, Anita." He had a smirk on his face. It reminded Anita of O.J. Simpson's smirk when the not-guilty verdict was read.

Barbara begged, "Don't come near us, Anita."

"No, I'm not letting Daryl hurt you." Gingerly, Anita stepped toward the two.

"No, Anita." Barbara turned toward Daryl again. Blood trickled down her chin. She wiped it with the back of her arm. "Daryl, we can solve this peacefully. Put the gun down. You don't need it. Daryl, don't do anything rash."

His bloodshot eyes pierced into Anita. "You're the one I want. I'll let her go if you take her place," he sneered. "Come here."

Slowly, Anita took a couple more steps in his direction. When she was within reach, he shoved Barbara out of the way. She tumbled into a chair. Daryl yanked Anita's left arm. She stumbled. In her peripheral vision she spotted a shadow on the deck; commotion.

Thunderous shots exploded.

FORTY

THE GUNSHOTS WERE DEAFENING. THERE WAS A crash from the shattered back sliding glass door. Dazed, Barbara fell off the chair to her hands and knees. *I hear sirens. They are louder now. Wait, if the police aren't here, who fired the shots from the back deck?*

Anita crumpled to the floor, her left arm wrapped around her side where she was shot. Daryl fell on top of her, blood pooling onto Anita's shirt. Anita pushed him and crawled out from under his heavy weight. He moaned and reached for her. Daryl's gun was lying on the floor next to them. Barbara, who was still on the floor near them, shoved it away.

The man lying on the deck just outside the shattered back slider was Bill Cratelli, the original private eye Daryl hired to find out if Anita was having an affair. And then, Daryl tried to hire him again when Anita disappeared. When Cratelli found out about the restraining order against Daryl, he told him he wouldn't take the case but sensed something was very wrong. On a hunch, he followed Daryl, this time to the public beach a few miles away from the Kirkland beach house. However, dressed in neatly pressed black slacks, black Stuart McGuire shoes and a long-sleeved buttoned up shirt, he thought it would be too conspicuous to follow Daryl too closely. He lost him when Daryl left the beach and entered the housing area on the top of the sandbank. When Cratelli spotted Anita at the top of the wooded steps, he knew that Daryl would be close by.

Blood spilled from Cratelli's abdomen. He rolled back and forth and groaned. He still had a tight grip on his gun. He forced his other hand into his wounded belly hoping to stop the bleeding. Crimson blood oozed through his shirt and between his fingers.

Daryl had shot Anita through the right side of her back. She lay dazed and hemorrhaging. Barbara scurried into the kitchen to call 911 then realized the phone was still off the hook. She picked it up. "Is this 911?"

"Yes."

"Hurry, there are three people shot. We need the police and an ambulance right away. Our address ..."

The dispatcher interrupted, "We have officers on their way already. I heard you mention a gun and then heard the shots. They should be there shortly. I'm calling for an ambulance now. Are you safe now?"

"My friend has been shot and two others. Please hurry."

"There are three people shot?"

"Yes."

"I'll call for another ambulance. They will be there soon. Can you get to the front door and unlock it?"

Barbara didn't hear the last instructions from the dispatcher because she dropped the phone on the counter. She thought Daryl may still try to harm Anita. She looked for a weapon in the kitchen and found the heavy cast iron 12-inch skillet on the stove, bringing back dreadful memories of her abusive childhood and what she had done to protect her mother and brother. With adrenal-fueled strength, she lifted the pan and hauled it into the family room. Daryl was crawling toward his gun. Barbara smashed the skillet down on his hand. He reeled over and grabbed Barbara by the leg with his left hand. Again, with brute strength, Barbara lifted the cast iron pan. She struck Daryl on the head. His body went limp. She collapsed on the carpet, releasing the blood-spattered pan from her violently shaking hands. She kicked Daryl's gun farther away from him.

Barbara turned her attention to Anita and crawled over to her. "Anita, where are you hurt?" Anita rolled over onto her side and took a gasping breath. "Get me something to stop the bleeding." Her voice came out raspy and forced.

There was thunderous rapping on the front door. A loud voice announced, "This is the police. Open up." Then, a rattle of the locked door handle. They repeated, "Open up. This is the police."

Barbara was slowing getting up off the carpet; her cooked spaghetti like legs barely able to support her. Suddenly she heard the crack of wood from the door.

Two officers appeared through the entryway, guns drawn. "This is the police."

Barbara let out a shuttering breath and kneeled back down near Anita.

The officers scanned the room first seeing Daryl, clearly shot in the upper torso, blood pooling on the carpet from his body and head. A gun lay on the carpet out of his reach. His body was in a contorted position. He wasn't moving. Anita was lying on her side. Her right casted arm was awkwardly sticking up at the ceiling. The officer who entered the house first and clearly in charge, Officer Perez, tilted his head toward his shoulder and spoke into his radio calling for backup and another ambulance.

There was broken glass all over the floor and a man on the deck with what appeared to be a gunshot wound to his abdomen. His gun was still clenched in his hand.

"Put the gun down," Officer Perez demanded aiming his pistol at his upper body. The other officer who was much younger, Officer Rodowski, also aimed his gun at the man on the deck. The man released it to the floor. Officer Rodowski walked to the gun and kicked it out of reach. "Hands where I can see them." Perez pulled out his handcuffs.

"Roll over." Perez nodded his head sideways at his partner. "I got this."

Rodowski looked down at Daryl. "Roll over," he ordered. Daryl did not respond. "Roll over." He repeated. Rodowski bent down next to him. He was not breathing.

Perez nodded his head sideways again and looked down the hallway. Rodowski disappeared.

On the deck the man said, "Wait … I'm Bill Cratelli, Santa Clara P.D., retired." His voice came out croaky, uneven. A claw seemed to have tightened his windpipe. He struggled to continue, "Now P.I. I have …" he rolled on his side, "… a license to carry." His eyes rolled back and he let out a huge moan. "In my wallet."

Perez glared at Cratelli and commanded, "Leave your hands where I can see them. Now roll over and put them behind your back." Cratelli groaned as he sluggishly rolled over. Perez handcuffed him.

Rodowski returned into the living room. "Clear," he announced as he walked over to Daryl.

Anita tried to sit up clutching her side. "We need a couple of ambulances."

"Ma'am, we've called for them. I need you to sit tight."

"I'm a doctor."

"Okay, I still need to you stay where you are."

Barbara was shivering. "Thank God you're here." With her shaking hands wrapped around her body she rubbed her arms up and down.

Rodowski, standing over Daryl, rapidly rattled off words and numbers through his shoulder radio. He turned toward Barbara, "Are you the one who called?"

"Yes."

Anita spoke, pointing to Daryl. "That's my husband, Daryl. He had a gun. There were shots. I think he was going to kill us." Anita stared at Perez, her throat constricted. She pushed air up her throat and repeated, "I'm a doctor. Let me see what I can do to help."

Rodowski said, "Ambulances are on the way."

"We should try to stop their bleeding now. Barbara, get some dish towels … for all of us."

Anita slowly sat up, her blouse splotched in blood. Her heart was sprinting in her chest. She looked at Daryl lying on the floor. Her head spun around and around like a kid's top. She pulled her fingers through her hair. Disbelief and bile washed up Anita's throat as she stared into her husband's dull fixed pupils.

Sirens, more sirens. A police sergeant entered the living room, his gun drawn.

Perez said, his voice direct and stiff, "Sergeant McDulley, we have three people shot. One outside on the deck, cuffed." He pointed to Daryl where he lay motionless, the last blood trickling from open wounds. "Too late to help him. If the ambulance doesn't get here soon, we're gonna lose another."

"No one else in the house, Sir," Rodowski said.

Pointing toward Cratelli, Perez said, "He says he's retired P.D." Cratelli winced in pain. The Sergeant turned his attention toward Barbara. "Let me help you onto the couch." He holstered his weapon. The other officers did too. He lifted Barbara under her armpits. "Are you all right?"

"Yes, but very shaken."

Out on the deck, Cratelli moaned and rolled from side to side. "I'm Bill Cratelli ..." His voice was now thready and uneven. Anita looked at Barbara and the officers said, "Get me some clean kitchen towels. I need them now. I have to help him."

They heard sirens. "The ambulance will be here shortly."

Anita, still in shock, stagger-crawled to the back deck. Tenderly but authoritatively, in her doctor voice, she said, "Lie still. Help is on the way." He groaned louder. She pleaded, "Please let me help this man. I can't let him bleed to death."

"Ma'am ..."

"I've got to stop his bleeding. He's handcuffed for Christ sake. He can't hurt me." She reached over to a patio chair and dragged off a pillow and pushed it into Cratelli's abdomen. She leaned close to Cratelli's face and spoke softly. "What's your name? How did you know to be here?" Cratelli rolled his head to one side and exhaled. "Stay with me. You have to. You just saved my life."

FORTY-ONE

At the hospital Bill Cratelli was wheeled into surgery. The doctors removed his damaged kidney. He was given a blood transfusion and sent to ICU.

The gunshot to Anita went through her back near her right side. Once it was determined that none of her vital organs were injured, she was cleaned up and sutured. She was admitted to the hospital for observation. Daryl was pronounced dead at the scene.

Anita visited Cratelli when he was transferred to a regular hospital room. "Bill, Bill Cratelli," she said as she walked into his room. "May I come in?"

"Sure," he said in a low voice, "but don't be offended if I don't get up. I'm hooked to a bunch of machines and IV's so I'm a little tethered to this bed right now."

"That's okay. I'm a doctor and you're not the first person I've seen married to an IV." She walked up to his bed. "How are you doing?"

"Well, I've been better. Lost a kidney but the doctors tell me I don't need it anyway."

"Yes, you have an extra one. People do fine with one kidney." The floor screeched as she pulled the wooden chair near the hospital bed. "I've got a lot of questions for you, Bill Cratelli."

"I bet you do. First, you can call me Bill. No need to be formal, considering," he paused, "considering what we've been through."

"That's good with me, Bill. I'm Dr. Anita Stone, but you already know that. You can call me Anita from now on."

ANITA SPENT THREE WEEKS WITH THE KIRKLANDS recovering.

Cratelli remained in the hospital for two weeks. Anita stopped in to check on him a couple of times.

Thomas and Barbara sold their beach house to Dr. Michael Johnson and Lily, the Colombo expert. Much to Dr. Johnson's chagrin, Lily told all of her friends about the shooting that had taken place in their new beach house.

Thomas and Anita hired a new orthopedic surgeon to join their practice so Thomas could retire. At his retirement party, Thomas announced that he and Barbara would be leaving for a three-month respite to their house in Maui. Before they left Thomas pulled Anita aside. "Are you going to be all right?"

"Yes," she answered, "I have a PI watching over me." She nodded her head toward Bill Cratelli.

"I see." Thomas said as he raised his bushy eyebrows. "I won't worry about you. He a good man."

Two Years Later

ANITA, DRESSED IN A TEA-LENGTH, IRIDESCENT-BLUE sheath, stood on the beach outside Thomas and Barbara's second home in Maui. Her right hand held a bouquet of white dendrobium orchids and Hawaiian greenery. With her left hand, she tenderly held onto the arm of Dr. Thomas Kirkland. He was dressed in a pale blue, open collared shirt and beige trousers. The two of them strolled barefoot on the powdery sand. The Pacific Ocean painted a bejeweled sapphire backdrop. Waiting for her under a white arbor decorated with citrusy sweet perfumed plumeria was Anita's matron-of-honor, Barbara. Beside her stood the groom. Around his neck hung a horseshoe shaped lei made of spice scented green maile stems and leaves. Bill Cratelli, dressed in khaki pants and a muted Hawaiian shirt, waited for his bride.

FROM THE AUTHOR

The question I am asked most often is why I wrote a book about domestic violence. I was a victim of domestic violence and although the people and events in this story are fictional, the premise of what happens in these types of relationships is not. Some people told me that they didn't think the audience would be big enough, or the story line would be too dramatic or too depressing for an entire book. I stuck to my original resolve hoping that by writing this book I could bring more awareness and conversation to this very serious, complicated, and convoluted problem. It affects many people, much more than is reported, and much more than you probably realize. Some of your friends, neighbors or co-workers may currently be victims. It can turn deadly; often does. Here's one staggering statistic from Domestic Violence Intervention Program www.dvipiowa.org. "Women are 70 times more likely to be killed in the two weeks after leaving a battering partner than at any other time in the relationship."

Domestic violence happens all around us, affecting not only the victim and abuser but their families, friends, first responders and employers.

I heard, "Why don't victims just leave?" It's much more complex than packing a suitcase and saying goodbye to someone you love. There are most certainly emotional ties. Victims told me their emotional scars ran deeper than their physical ones. Abusers are adept at pulling heartstrings and demeaning their victims. There are financial concerns in a great many of these situations, but even if that is not the case, the situation is precarious at best and may be deadly. Sometimes victims are too embarrassed thinking they have somehow caused this abuse or they deserved it. When I was in this situation I was embarrassed. How could I have gotten myself into this? I was monumentally afraid.

Growing up, I heard and read about domestic violence but erroneously thought that it only happened to others. I wondered how someone could be so blind as to stay in a relationship with someone who abuses them. I stereotyped the type of person who was a victim. It certainly wasn't a Caucasian physician, as in my story.

I have since learned domestic violence does not discriminate based on color, religion, education, salary, or job title. Victims may be homeless or live in a mansion. They may be a drug addict or a doctor writing the prescriptions. They may a housekeeper or a CEO, a movie star or famous athlete, gay or straight.

Many resources are available now. Victims need access and exposure to those resources as well as a safe plan to get out. Abusers need help too. So do the families and friends involved. Education is vital, starting at a young age.

- What are the early warning signs that

someone will abuse or be a victim?

- What can we do to stop it?
- Why do we tolerate bullying and disrespect?
- When teachers notice bullying or abusive traits at an early age, what can be done?
- Is there anything you can do to help?

No More is my contribution to bringing domestic violence more to the forefront. It takes place during the first two weeks after Dr. Anita Stone leaves her abusive husband. This is the time when things are very volatile and more likely deadly. I created these characters with the victim a doctor because I believe almost anyone can be fooled by an abuser. There are upsetting events that happen in the characters' lives. We are not born to be abusers or victims. The circumstances and events in our lives contribute to our future path.

My hope is that with discussion, awareness, education, and resources, we can all help end the cycle of abuse.

WHERE TO GET HELP

National Domestic Violence Hotline
www.thehotline.org 1-800-799-7233 (24 hours)

National Sexual Assault Hotline
www.rainn.org 1-800-656-HOPE (4673)
National Sexual Assault is the largest anti-sexual
assault organization in the United States.

National Teen Dating Abuse Helpline
www.loveisrepect.org 866-331-9474
Teens and parents anywhere in the country can call or
log on to the interactive website.

NOMORE.org
No More is dedicated to getting the issues of
domestic violence, sexual assault, and abuse out of the
shadows.

ACKNOWLEDGMENTS

No More would not have gotten off the ground without the encouragement and support of my Thursday morning writing teacher, Susan Wilson. She created a positive, nurturing atmosphere where my fellow writers and I could gather, learn, read, and cheer each other on so our voices—our unique styles of writing—could be explored and enhanced. Thank you, Susan, and all my fellow students for listening, sharing your stories, your optimism, and your friendship.

There are three special women writers in my life who have made the journey of writing this novel with me. We call ourselves the W-4. We've met almost twice a month for a couple years critiquing, analyzing, and sharing our work, our friendship, food and wine. Susan Reid, thank you for your creative energy and thoughtful critique. Leslie Haas, thank you for your editing skills, your open and honest opinions, your humor, and coming up with interesting vegetable recipes, even though you are not a fan.

Marilyn Dumesnil, my awarding-winning poet friend, thank you for introducing me to your beautiful, flowing poetry and contributing "Hidden Fire" to my book. Thank you for your words of wisdom, helping me get through the times when I did not want to write, needed a break, or didn't feel the manuscript was good enough. You encouraged me to listen to my inner voice when I needed a break and to quiet that same voice when it was being too critical. This book would not have been completed without these three women.

I want to thank another three beautiful souls, my yoga instructors from Livermore Valley Tennis Club, Donna Manning, Katherine Kozioziemski and Laura Ragan. Each of you provided a calming, a centering for me when *No More* became too intense. For your guidance in my yoga journey, thank you.

I am immensely grateful to my husband, Steve, my rock and my security. He is the epitome of respectfulness and strength.

ABOUT THE AUTHOR

When Antoinette Foxworthy was thirty-nine, she quit her human resources job in Silicon Valley to move next door to Craigdarroch Castle in Victoria, British Colombia, so she could spend more time developing her craft. She has won awards for her short stories and poetry. *No More* is her debut novel.

The mother of four grown daughters, her passions include traveling, reading, writing, yoga, taking her famous "My Perspective" pictures, and anything related to her eight grandchildren. She and her husband Steve currently live in Northern California.

Antoinette is available for readings. To learn more about Antoinette, read some of her poetry, short stories, or see some of her famous "My Perspective" photographs, please visit her website at www.afoxworthy.com.

CPSIA information can be obtained
at www.ICGtesting.com
Printed in the USA
FSOW01n1128111117
40998FS